ANNIE'S ATTIC MYSTERIES®

The Key in the Attic

DeAnna Julie Dodson

Annie's®
AnniesFiction.com

The Key in the Attic
Copyright © 2012, 2016 Annie's.

The characters and events in this book are fictional, and any resemblance to actual persons or events is coincidental.

Library of Congress-in-Publication Data
The Key in the Attic / by DeAnna Julie Dodson
p. cm.
I. Title
2012905427

AnniesFiction.com
800-282-6643
Annie's Attic Mysteries®
Series Editors: Ken and Janice Tate
Series Creator: Stenhouse & Associates, Ridgefield, Connecticut

10 11 12 13 14 | Printed in China | 9 8 7 6

~ 1 ~

"Alice, look out!"

Annie Dawson grabbed her best friend's arm and dragged her back just as A Stitch in Time's front window shattered. Behind them, the women of the Hook and Needle Club shrieked and threw up their hands to shield their faces from flying glass.

An instant later, everything was still along Stony Point's Main Street. Everyone could only stare, openmouthed, at the front of the neon-yellow Porsche convertible that was now jammed under two racks of crochet patterns and a pile of worsted weight yarn. After a frozen moment, the young driver scrambled out of the front seat and into the shop, hot-pink cellphone still in hand.

"Oh wow—oh wow." The girl looked around at the wreckage, her blond ponytail bobbing behind her. "Oh wow—my mom's gonna kill me!"

"Are you all right?" Annie asked her, and then she turned to the other women. "Is everybody all right?"

Behind the swell of chatter from the rest of ladies, Stella calmly finished counting stitches, put her knitting in her lap and pushed her reading glasses down so she could look at the girl over them. "Is that Amanda Culbertson?"

The girl's eyes got even rounder than they had been. "Y-yes, Mrs. Brickson, it is. I'm so sorry. I don't know what happened. I was just driving and all of a sudden—"

"You were just talking on that phone of yours and not paying attention." Stella glanced at the telltale device and then back at the girl's guilty face. "Or was it texting this time? I know your grandmother has talked to you about that more than once."

"Oh please, Mrs. Brickson, *please* don't tell her or my mom and dad that part. I know I'm not supposed to. I just looked away for a second, I promise."

"You're lucky you didn't hurt yourself or someone else." Annie's green eyes flashed, and she could have shaken the girl, but instead she led her to one of the circle of over-stuffed chairs that was set up for the needleworking club. "You'd better sit down for a minute and catch your breath before you call your parents."

"What was that!"

Hearing Mary Beth Brock's voice from the door that led to the basement, Annie glanced at Alice and then forced a note of cheerfulness into her own voice. "Nobody's hurt. Don't worry."

"But A Stitch in Time now has a drive-through," Alice MacFarlane called out, but her quip lightened the tension for only a moment.

When Mary Beth, the owner of A Stitch in Time, came into the front of her shop, the look on her face silenced everyone. Her shoulders drooped as she surveyed bolts of fabric, how-to books, and expertly stitched shop samples covered with glass fragments and smeared with grime from the still-running Porsche. Even her usually cheerful round face seemed to sag. The only sound she seemed to be able to manage was a bewildered little "oh."

Annie went to her side, and Kate Stevens, Mary Beth's shop assistant, hurried to her other side.

"Nobody's hurt," Kate assured her. "And I don't think there's too much damage. Besides the window of course. Some of our inventory ..."

She trailed off, seeing Mary Beth wasn't really hearing her.

Amanda ducked her blond head and hunched her slim, T-shirt-clad shoulders. Then she looked pleadingly up at Mary Beth. "I'm really sorry, Miss Brock. I didn't mean to. I promise I'll help clean everything up. And we have good insurance. I wasn't, um ..."

She, too, became silent. Mary Beth didn't seem to notice. Practical Peggy Carson went out and turned off the humming Porsche.

Annie gave Mary Beth a sturdy hug. "We'll get it all put right. You'll see. I think it's just broken glass, and I bet Peggy can get Wally over here in no time to board up that window until it can be replaced."

"Sure I can," Peggy said, her smile encouraging, as she returned the Porsche's keys to its flustered driver. "In fact, I'll call him right now. It's such a nice spring day anyway. A little fresh air won't hurt anything."

Annie glanced again at Alice. This wasn't at all like Mary Beth. She'd faced her share of hard times and unexpected difficulties, but she had always met them with resolute determination and practicality.

"Sure." Mary Beth nodded. "Sure. You're not hurt are you, Amanda?"

The girl shook her head and then made an attempt at a smile. "At least not till Mom hears about this."

Again Mary Beth nodded blankly. Then she slumped down into a chair and burst into tears.

* * * *

"I think Mary Beth is in trouble," said Kate when the five friends sat down at the Formica-topped table at The Cup & Saucer. Annie looked first at Alice, who was sitting beside her, and then she looked back across the table at Kate.

"I'm glad I'm not the only one worried about her, Kate," Annie said. "She hasn't been herself lately, and she was way too upset about Mandy Culbertson crashing into her front window yesterday. I could understand her being mad about it. If that happened to me, my hair would be a lot more gray than blond. But I've never seen Mary Beth cry like that over anything."

Kate sighed. "I know she's been having a hard time, like everybody has in this economy, but I think it's more than that now. The window was just the last straw. She has had to cancel some orders for the shop more and more often these days." She toyed with the little cow-shaped saltshaker, not looking up. "And she's cut way back on my work hours."

A general murmur of sympathy went around the group of women jammed into the back booth at the diner.

"No, no, I'm not worried about me." Kate smiled a little wryly. "Not much anyway. Harry has been pretty regular with the child support lately, and I've been doing really well selling my patterns for crocheted jackets and things. But

I don't know about Mary Beth. She's been ... . Well, she'd
never complain, you know, but I can tell she's struggling.
That's why I wanted to get everybody together today. I just
thought there ought to be some way we can help her out.
She's been really good to me for a long time now."

"She's been good to all of us," Alice said, her blue eyes
flashing. "It's not right that the best people always seem to
have the hardest time. I'm glad you told us about this, Kate."

"You don't think she might lose A Stitch in Time do
you? What would we do without our needlework shop?"
Gwendolyn Palmer, sitting in the opposite corner of the
booth, shook her head. "I thought Mary Beth seemed a
little distracted when we had our club meeting last week,
but I didn't think it was anything serious. I just assumed
her sister was giving her a hard time again."

Peggy rolled her eyes. "Her sister."

An elderly couple came into the restaurant, and Peggy
glanced over to make sure one of the other waitresses was
taking care of them. Then she turned back to her friends,
one hand on her plump, pink-uniformed hip. "I mean,
you'd think Miss World-Renowned Fashion Designer
Melanie would be able to help her sister out once in a
while," said Peggy.

"I doubt Melanie even knows about it," Annie rea-
soned. "We didn't know about it, and we're Mary Beth's best
friends. Do you know all this for sure, Kate?"

Kate shrugged a little. "Only that she's cut down on
my hours and had to cancel some orders for merchandise.
Come to think of it, I did hear her on the phone last week
about some antique furniture. First I assumed she was

wanting to buy it, but now I'm wondering if she was having to sell something of her own."

A woman and two children came in and sat down at the lunch counter, and Peggy took a quick glance at her watch. "My break's almost over, ladies. If we're going to decide something, we'd better do it quick."

"Don't be too hasty now." Stella had sat silently in the corner ever since she had arrived, but she had taken in every word. "We would all like to help Mary Beth in any way we can, but it has to be done the right way. She wouldn't want us to pity her or think she doesn't know how to manage her own affairs."

"We'd want to be discreet," Annie said. "There's no need for the whole town to know her personal business."

Kate blushed. "I never would have said anything, you know, but I was worried that—"

"Of course you should have told *us*," Alice assured her. "We can't let anything happen to Mary Beth. Stony Point wouldn't be the same without her and A Stitch in Time."

"We wouldn't even have the Hook and Needle Club," Peggy said, a little quiver in her lip.

Annie squeezed her arm. "Now, nothing's happened yet, Peggy. And we're not going to let anything happen to Mary Beth, are we, girls?"

"Of course not," Alice said over the determined murmuring of the others.

"We could have a bake sale," Gwen suggested, but Stella shook her head.

"That would be very nice, dear, but not likely to be much help in a case like this."

"What about a real fundraiser?" Kate asked. "I mean, really get some things together and have an auction or something. We've done them before for other causes." She glanced at Alice, remembering when the group came together to help when her business went through a rough time. "Why not for Mary Beth? We all have stuff we don't really need."

Stella looked wary about the idea, and Annie had to agree. "We can't do something public like that. We don't want to embarrass Mary Beth."

Peggy sighed.

"Well, something private then." Alice's eyes sparkled. "As Kate said, we all have things we don't really need or use. Why not take some of the nice things to see what we can get for them."

Annie grinned. "That's a great idea. You know Gram has a ton of stuff in the attic. Some of it is antique and may be worth a little. I don't think there is anything that extremely valuable, but enough to help Mary Beth until she gets past whatever's going on. And Gram would love to know it was used for someone she loved."

"We don't all have an attic full of treasures like you," Peggy said with another sigh.

"Don't you worry, Peg," Kate assured her. "We can all do something."

"And everything will be from all of us," Annie insisted. "Deal?"

Annie slapped her hand down on the table, and all the other women piled theirs on top. All except one—Stella still looked unconvinced.

"I just don't know how Mary Beth will feel about this," she said. "Maybe someone should talk to her first."

Everyone looked at Annie, and she gave the older woman an encouraging smile.

"We'll figure out some way to handle it that won't embarrass her, OK?"

Stella looked at all the expectant faces around her and finally added her hand to the others.

"All right."

*   *   *   *

It seemed that no matter how many things she took out of it, there were always more in the attic of Grey Gables that Annie hadn't gone through yet. There were plenty of things she could sell—antiques and oddities and lovely bits of the past. One of her favorites was a carved elephant, perhaps a foot tall, exquisitely fashioned out of ivory and what looked like teak. It had to be over a hundred years old, maybe much older, and from some exotic place. She ran her fingers longingly over its glass-smooth surface and then put it in the cardboard box she was filling.

"I've lived without you my entire life up until now, Mr. Elephant. I think I can struggle on without you in the future."

A little more rummaging brought to light six silver teaspoons in a baroque rose pattern, black with neglect, and she put them into the box too.

"A little polish will make you look good as new. And you."

She added a silver chafing dish and matching serving

spoon. They were much newer than the teaspoons, but still very nice.

By dinnertime, she had filled two good-sized boxes with potential sale items, and she was pleased with what she had found so far: leather-bound classic books she hoped would turn out to be first editions, a pretty cloisonné dresser set from the 1920s, one of those painted cast-iron banks from the latter part of the nineteenth century, and several other items from a variety of times and places. All of it was lovely, and she hoped, reasonably valuable. But none of it was doing anyone any good up in the attic. She just hoped what she and the others could gather up would be enough to make a difference for Mary Beth. And she hoped they could figure out a way to get her to accept their help.

"One more thing ought to finish this one off," she decided, looking into the second box. "Something not too big."

She rummaged through a drawer in an old dresser and then closed it again. She wasn't giving up any of Gram's handwork—not unless it was an emergency. A battered suitcase offered nothing but a moth-eaten old tuxedo and some sheet music. Annie grinned, wondering about the story behind it; but knowing there was no monetary value in it, she shut the case once more.

Frowning, she looked around the attic. A small china vase sitting next to some crates on the floor caught her eye. It looked old and fragile, the roses and cherubs painted on it faded but still visible. It was perhaps ten inches tall—twelve inches including the little metal stand that held it—and only four or five inches wide. It was a sweetly graceful reminder of another time.

She wavered as she examined it. It would look very nice on the mantelpiece next to Gram's wedding picture. Then she shook her head and put it into the box with the other things.

"I can get along nicely without you, too, no matter how pretty you are."

Who knew? Maybe it would turn out to be worthless, and then she would keep it after all.

She picked up the box with the vase sticking out of the top, and started down the attic stairs. Before she had taken even two steps, she heard a mournful cry from the other side of the door.

"No," Annie called. "I told you that you couldn't come up here, and I meant it."

The cry was repeated, even more pathetically this time, and then the door rattled in its frame. Annie could see her cat's little white-tipped paw underneath it.

"Yes, Boots, I know it's dinnertime. I'm coming. I'm coming."

She tried to get a firmer grip on the box as she hurried down and stumbled as she did. A brief vision of herself tumbling helplessly to the bottom of the steps flashed before her eyes, but she managed to shift her weight backward in time to prevent a fall. The delicate china vase wavered in the top of the box before toppling over the edge, and she scrambled to hold onto it and the box. Unable to do both at the same time, she could only cringe at the crash that announced the vase's untimely demise.

Taking each step with extra caution, Annie made her way down to the attic door. She couldn't hear anything out in the hallway anymore.

"Scaredy cat," she called, but she was glad the crash had spooked Boots. No need getting glass in any curious little paws.

She set the box on the bottom step and sat next to it with the fragmented remains of the vase at her feet. She told herself it probably wouldn't have brought much in a sale anyway, but she had liked it. There was something very sweet about it—as innocent as first love. It was as easily shattered too.

With a sigh, she started picking up the larger pieces. It couldn't possibly be fixed. Too much of it lay in glistening little shards and slivers on the wooden floor. The metal stand was still intact, of course, but it looked as if part of it had come loose.

Annie picked it up. No, the stand was fine. What she was seeing was some kind of brass fitting that had been stuck to the bottom of the vase with putty. When she had examined the vase earlier, she had thought the putty was to secure the vase in its stand. Now it looked as if—

A *key*.

She wriggled it loose from its hiding place. The putty was hard and brittle now, broken like the vase, and the key quickly came free.

It was an odd-looking little thing, maybe an inch long, maybe smaller, but rather heavy for its size. It looked as if it was made of brass, and instead of the usual flourishes or loops, the bow was ornamented with the head of a lion.

She turned it over in her hand and then over again. "What I wouldn't give to know what you went to. Maybe a diary or a travel case or something that is probably long gone by now."

The door rattled again, and Annie stuffed the key into the pocket of her jeans.

"All right, scaredy cat. I'm coming."

~ 2 ~

The following Tuesday morning, Annie was the last to arrive at the meeting of the Hook and Needle Club. Everyone else was huddled together next to one of the pattern racks, and Kate motioned her over to them.

"Mary Beth's down in the basement getting a packet of appliqué needles for Peggy, so we just have a minute. Did you find anything good up in your attic?"

Annie dumped her purse and crochet bag into an unoccupied chair. "Several promising things. What about all of you? And—hey!—Wally did a great job getting that window taken care of. You can't tell anything ever happened."

"If there's one thing my Wally knows, it's putting stuff back the way it's supposed to be." Peggy's eyes sparkled. "I didn't think he and I would be able to do anything much to help Mary Beth. Wally offered to do the window for free, but she wouldn't let him. Anyway, Wally has some baseball cards he's kept since he was a boy—some he got from his grandpa—and he thinks they might be worth something. He said he doesn't mind helping Mary Beth with them if they are."

Gwen nodded and whispered, "I have this really old—"

"It must be good if you're whispering," interrupted Mary Beth.

Mary Beth laughed as she came up to them, and panicked,

the other women looked at Annie. Scrambling for something plausible to say, Annie pulled her key ring out of her pocket and showed Mary Beth the little key that had been plastered under the bottom of the china vase in the attic.

"I accidentally broke one of Gram's vases the other day, and this was stuck underneath it. I don't know what it goes to, and I just thought I'd see if anybody had any ideas."

Mary Beth studied it for a moment. "That's funny. That lion looks just like the ones that are on my end table at home."

Annie frowned. "Aw, and I was hoping it was something really old and mysterious."

Mary Beth laughed. "If it goes with the table, it *is* old. That thing was passed down at least from my great-great-grandmother's time. It's just a table though. Nothing to open up. No locks. May I see it?"

Annie slipped the key off the ring and handed it to Mary Beth.

"Definitely looks like the lions on my table. And it was stuck underneath a vase?"

Annie nodded. "It looked like it had been covered up with some kind of putty, and then the vase was stuck onto a metal stand."

"I wonder … ." Mary Beth's eyes narrowed. "I'm just wondering, if this *is* connected to my table somehow, how did it get stuck to the vase? And how did the vase end up in Betsy's attic?"

"You know how Gram was. She was a collector, and she liked pretty and interesting things."

"And people liked giving them to her," Alice added.

"Who knows how it ended up in the attic?"

Mary Beth thought for a minute more. "Wait a minute. The vase you broke, was it kind of tall and delicate with flowers and little angels painted on it?"

Annie nodded, a little spark of anticipation running through her.

"And it was on a brass stand, wasn't it?"

Again Annie nodded. "At least I think it's brass."

"Then I'm sure Mother must have given that to your grandmother. Betsy was one of the few people besides me who visited my mother at Seaside Hills Assisted Living before she died."

"Really? I wish there was something left of it so you could look at it. It broke into a million pieces."

"That's all right. Mother gave it to me a long time ago. Then, when she went to assisted living, I took it to her with some flowers in it. I always wondered what happened to it—not that it was worth much of anything."

"I'm sorry, Mary Beth. I wish I'd known. I would've given it back to you."

Mary Beth patted Annie's arm. "Don't you worry about it. I'm sure Mother was glad Betsy had it. I know she enjoyed the visits."

"But if the key and the table both were in your family, doesn't that prove they go together?" Peggy clasped her hands together. "How exciting! A secret key."

"That doesn't really prove anything, you know," Stella said. "Maybe a long while back there was another piece of furniture, something matching, something that had a lock. Mary Beth says the table doesn't have one."

Peggy wrinkled her nose. "You're no fun."

"Is there another piece?" Kate asked, and Mary Beth shook her head.

"Not that I ever heard of. There was the table with the lions on it, another table with chairs in a different style, a writing desk, some china, a mantel clock and some silver pieces passed down from my great-great-grandmother, but that's all, besides a few books and papers. I—uh—don't have the desk anymore, but the fittings on it weren't anything like this key."

Annie glanced at Kate. Was the writing desk the antique piece Kate had overheard Mary Beth trying to sell? Annie and the rest of the club had to do something quickly before Mary Beth was forced to let go of any other family treasures.

"Hmmm."

Alice nudged Annie out of her reverie. "Are you going to stare at that key all day, or are we going to do our hook-and-needle thing?"

Laughing, she and the others went to their places in the circle of chairs.

"Here are your needles, Peggy." Mary Beth handed her the little black and gold paper packet she had brought up from the basement. "And, Annie, you're welcome to come look at my great-great-grandma's table if you would like. I don't know if it'll help."

"You know me." Annie gave her a smile. "Leave no mystery unsolved."

"Yes, we definitely know you. Come by my place after the shop closes tonight. OK, everybody, before we get started, how about we each give an update on the projects we're working on. Gwen, why don't you start us off? That's a gorgeous sweater you're knitting. I love that teal and gold blend."

*   *   *   *

Mary Beth's cottage was much like her: warm and welcoming, unpretentious, neatly kept and eclectic. As always, a picture of her beloved niece had a prominent place on her mantel.

"This is a new one, isn't it?" Annie smiled as she looked at the pretty young woman with expressive blue eyes and long blonde hair. "How is Amy these days?"

"Oh, busy-busy as usual, but she's promised me a visit soon." Mary Beth's dark eyes glowed. "I have so many things planned for when she's here. I may even close the shop for a few days, just so we'll have time together."

"Couldn't Kate—"

"Kate's been pretty busy herself these days with her pattern sales and all. I hate to keep her tied down to the shop."

Or can't afford to.

"Mary Beth ... um, how *is* the shop lately?"

The older woman merely made an airy gesture with both hands. "Oh, ups and downs as always. You used to help your husband with your car dealership, didn't you? You know how it is. Do you want some coffee?"

Annie held back a wry smile. So much for finding out more about Mary Beth's financial problems.

"That would be great."

She glanced around the room once Mary Beth had left it. The living room window, hung with sweet floral-patterned drapes, overlooked a garden bursting with white wild-oats, showy blue harebells, and purple columbine, but the lovely cherry writing desk that had once stood in front of it was gone. An afghan-draped rocking chair now stood in its place. What else had she been forced to sell just to stay solvent?

Annie finally turned to the object of her visit: the gleaming round walnut table that stood at the end of Mary Beth's sofa. The top was perhaps twenty inches across. The apron around it was four or five inches deep, and as Mary Beth had said, brass lion heads that matched the key were placed at regular intervals around it, connected by intricately carved swags of flower garlands. The tabletop rested on a six-sided pedestal mounted on a base shaped almost like a six-pointed star, the gentle inward curves coming out to blunted points that rested on clawed feet. Like the top, the pedestal and base were lavishly carved.

Annie got down on her knees so she could see underneath the tabletop. Obviously, the apron was strictly for ornamental purposes, because there were no inner workings to conceal. All the space inside was hollow.

"This is really a beautiful table." Annie got back to her feet when Mary Beth returned with the coffee. "I'd never really noticed it when I was here before. But I see what you mean about there not being any drawers or anything."

Mary Beth handed her a steaming cup. "It's been in the family a long, long time. I think if it held any secrets, we'd know about it by now. Maybe there was a matching piece that got sold or thrown out years ago."

Annie breathed in the rich smell of the coffee, grappling with her disappointment. Then she set the cup down on the mantel, leaving it untasted.

"You know I can't leave it like that. Would you mind if I turned the table over and gave it a really good look?"

Mary Beth laughed and cleared the table of the few pictures and knickknacks that decorated it. Annie got down on her knees again and turned it onto its side and then onto its top.

"No keyhole here," she reported as she examined the base. "I thought maybe there'd be one right in the middle here, but it's only a wooden peg."

Mary Beth didn't say anything, but there was an I-could-have-told-you-that-much twinkle in her eye.

Undaunted, Annie lay the table on its side again and rapped on one of the pedestal's six sides.

"It's hollow."

"Most likely," Mary Beth said, "but you can't get into it without taking the whole thing apart."

Annie examined the carving, searching from one side to the next to the next, looking for anything that looked even slightly different from the rest. Finally she sat back.

"You can't get into it unless you have a key—" She grinned at Mary Beth. "—and a keyhole."

"Did you find something? No way!"

"Look right here."

Mary Beth got down on the floor beside Annie and squinted.

"Wait a minute."

A few seconds later, she was back, her reading glasses perched on her nose.

"Now show me what you mean."

"Right there." Annie pointed out a tiny carved rose, perhaps an eighth of an inch across, that was surrounded by a dozen others just like it. "See? It's got this little channel all the way around it. And this leaf ... see there, right next to it? It's split down the middle like all the other ones, but the split on this one goes all the way through. What if ...?" She took the key from her pocket and examined it. "What if the hollow end of this key fits *over* this rose and the bit slides right into the leaf?"

She tried it as she said it. The fit was snug, but the key went in.

Mary Beth's eyes were round. "Oh Annie!"

Annie's heart was pattering a mile a minute, and she had to bite her lip to keep from laughing.

"Maybe you should open it, Mary Beth. It's yours."

"Oh no. I'd be so excited that I'd break something. Go ahead."

"Are you sure?"

"Open it! Open it!"

Annie took a deep breath. "Here goes."

Her fingers trembling, she turned the key. There was a tiny click, but nothing else happened.

Mary Beth huffed in exasperation. Annie glanced at her and then gave the key a tug.

The whole side of the pedestal came loose.

Mary Beth had both hands over her mouth, her eyes even rounder than before. "I don't believe it!"

"It's hollow like you said, but it's not empty." Annie handed her a little paper packet tied up with string. "Protected from light and air like that, it looks like it's in pretty good shape, but it must be very old."

Mary Beth turned it over. "I'm almost afraid to touch it, but I'm dying to know what it says."

Annie bit her lip. "It's just tied in a bow. If you give it the tiniest little pull ..."

Mary Beth did. The string came off easily, and she gently lifted one corner of the packet and then a second.

Annie reached inside. "There's another key. What does the paper say?"

Mary Beth sat down on the couch and laid the pages on the coffee table so she could examine them more closely. Annie sat beside her.

"Look at that copperplate handwriting. It must be very old."

Mary Beth shook her head. "I really can't believe this."

"What does it say?"

Mary Beth passed the pages to Annie so she could read them for herself.

Beloved Angeline,

A letter brought you here, and now you must find more:

England's 45 inches
Twice indebted
Katherine at home

Blue and twinkling
Roadside refuge

Turn to the right
Twice beholden

Scotland's river

Busy sweets maker
Twice obliged
Katherine to her friends

50~2~4~1
1~1~1~1
2~32~16~11
19~23~5~4
62~1~5~21
19~27~1~1
18~11~8~11
5~29~29~2
19~119~114~5

Yours always,
Geoffrey

"A real puzzle," Annie said. "And I bet it's at least a hundred years old—maybe a hundred and fifty. How fun is that?"

Mary Beth shook her head again. "I really can't believe this. My great-great-grandmother's name was Angeline. It has to have been meant for her."

"Oh, how sweet. Your great-great-grandfather must have left this puzzle for her. I wonder what it leads to and where he hid the other letters and what this new key goes to."

"No, it couldn't have been him. Yes, my great-great-grandmother was Angeline, but my great-great-grandfather's name was James."

"Then who was Geoffrey?"

— 3 —

Annie still stared at the note. *Beloved Angeline.* There was a sweet tenderness in the way he had written the name. Yet somehow he and his beloved had not ended up spending their lives together. Why?

Mary Beth wrinkled her forehead. "I've never heard the mention of a Geoffrey in the family—not that I remember." She paused for a moment. "Wait a second."

"If you don't mind, I'm going to make a copy of this clue so we won't mess up the original," Annie said, digging in her purse for her notepad as her friend disappeared down the hallway.

"OK," Mary Beth called back. "Thanks for thinking of it."

Annie was writing down the last string of numbers and trying to make some sense of them when Mary Beth came back into the room looking a little disheveled. She had a metal file box in her hands.

"Sorry that took so long. I had to move some things around to get to the right box." She smiled. "Mother had all this just stuffed in a drawer when we cleaned out her house before she moved to Seaside. I'm glad I could rescue all of it. She never was very sentimental; I'm surprised she didn't throw this out years ago."

She sat beside Annie on the couch, clicked the latch on the box, and swung its lid back on its hinges.

Annie looked inside, feeling that little quickening of her pulse that came any time she got a chance to see bits of what people had left behind them, things they had found dear enough to keep and then pass to their loved ones.

Mary Beth started removing items, carefully, one by one, mindful of a delicate bit of writing or an already-cracked daguerreotype. There were letters and deeds and a pair of old miniatures—portraits, Annie imagined—of an aunt and uncle many times removed. A small book of prayer was nestled in between a little rag doll and a well-used account book. There was nothing of any monetary value, but everything in this box had some special meaning, Annie was sure. The interesting part was figuring out each item's significance.

"Here it is."

Mary Beth pulled out a little booklet, no bigger than her hand, decorated with a pinkish gray tassel that must have once been a vivid red. Inside was a program for a cotillion held on the third day of March in 1861. The lines beside each of the dances had been penciled in with the names of a variety of gentlemen. Most of the writing was smudged and faded now, but only one name was repeated more than once: G. Whyte. At the bottom in flowing script was written "Miss Angeline Morrow."

"G. Whyte." Annie breathed a sigh quietly. "It could be Geoffrey, couldn't it? Does the signature look like the writing in the note?"

She and Mary Beth both leaned over the coffee table, squinting at the precise copperplate letters, comparing them to what was written on the dance card.

"It's hard to say." Mary Beth frowned. "That could be

the same G, I suppose. Whoever wrote on the dance card looks as if he was in a hurry."

Annie chuckled. "He's on there four times. He must have wanted to make sure he got to dance with her."

Mary Beth laughed too. "I suppose."

"Look at the 'h' and 't' in 'brought' in the note. And look at the way they are in 'Whyte.' I think they must be written by the same hand. The 'y' in both places he wrote 'you' look very similar to the ones on the dance card. It must be the same person."

Mary Beth's smile turned a little sad. "They must have had a falling out since he's not the one she married."

"Yes," Annie sighed. "Still, we don't know. The early spring of 1861 was right before the Civil War. Maybe he was killed in battle."

"Oh, that's even sadder."

"We'll have to see if we can find out something about him. I've done a little genealogical research before. You'd be surprised the kind of things they put on the Internet." Annie finished jotting down the last part on her notepad, adding notes from the dance card. "We can at least solve the puzzle he left behind."

Mary Beth peered through her reading glasses at the note to Angeline. "I can't make heads or tails out of it. Do you suppose each line of writing goes with each line of numbers? Maybe each number stands for a letter that spells out a word. Like one equals A, two equals B and so on."

Annie swiftly counted the lines. "Nope. No such luck. There are eleven lines of word clues and only nine lines of numbers. And each of the number lines only have four numbers in it. Besides, the numbers go way too high to stand for the alphabet."

Mary Beth frowned. "I don't seem to be that great with numbers lately anyway."

Annie kept her eyes on the brittle yellow page. "It's not easy being in business these days. I'm glad I don't have to worry about the car dealership anymore."

"At least you had Wayne to shoulder a lot of the load."

"Most of it, if you want the truth." Annie glanced up at her friend. "If I had tried to keep the dealership after he died, I would have had a hard time doing everything on my own. I don't know how you keep things going at the shop all by yourself."

"Not very well. Not lately."

"You have a lot of friends to help you. We'd all be happy to—"

"Don't be silly. Businesses go through bad patches. That's just normal. Either they stay afloat or they don't. That's normal too."

"But Mary Beth—"

"I said don't be silly." Mary Beth cleared her throat and got that no-nonsense look Annie was very familiar with. "Now we have a puzzle to solve."

The two of them bandied around ideas for a while over more coffee and some pecan tarts Mary Beth had brought home, left over from the latest church supper. Annie had hoped there would be something else in Mary Beth's box of family memorabilia that would help them solve the puzzle, but there was nothing.

"It's probably something obvious," Mary Beth said, and

then an enormous yawn escaped her. "Oh, excuse me. I don't know where that came from."

Annie smiled and stood up. "I think that's my cue to go home and let you get some rest."

"It's early. I never go to bed at this hour."

Annie put her coffee cup and her plate in the sink. "You've had a lot on your mind, Mary Beth. Some extra sleep is probably just what you need."

"But—"

"No buts, now. I'll take my notes home with me. Maybe something will come to me on the way there. If not, I'll get Alice to have a look too. She's bound to have some good ideas." Annie gave Mary Beth a wink. "Maybe the answer will come to you in a dream."

Mary Beth laughed. "Then I guess I'd better try to get some sleep."

*   *   *   *

"Did you find something? Let me see!"

As soon as Annie pulled her classic Malibu into the driveway at Grey Gables, Alice scooted out of the carriage house next door and hurried up the hill to meet her. Alice's blue eyes were sparkling, obviously eager to know if the little key had actually unlocked some mystery at Mary Beth's house.

"Let me get the door unlocked." Annie fumbled with her key and finally turned the lock. "Go on in the kitchen. Start some coffee, please, if you don't mind. Let me check my messages and feed Boots, and then I'll tell you all about it."

"Now you're torturing me," Alice complained, but

she hurried toward the kitchen. "You did find something, though, didn't you?"

"Just hang on. I'll be right there."

The only message on Annie's voicemail was a portion of an automated political survey. She promptly pressed the delete key and went into the kitchen. Boots was already pacing by her empty food bowl. Annie put her purse in a chair and opened the cabinet where she kept the dry cat food.

"OK, OK, Miss Boots. I'm coming."

"She probably just wants to know what happened at Mary Beth's too," Alice said as she filled the coffeepot with tap water.

Annie dumped a scoop of crunchy seafood-flavored cat food into Boots's bowl and then got two large coffee cups out of the cabinet on the other side of the coffeemaker.

"I'll do that," Alice said, shooing Annie toward the big table in the middle of the kitchen. "You start talking."

"OK. The key did open up the pedestal of her antique table, and there was this note inside." Annie took her copy of the clue out of her purse and spread it out on the table. "We think it's from sometime around the Civil War."

Alice lifted one dark brow. "They had bright orange note paper during the Civil War?"

"Very funny. This is what I copied down. Mary Beth has the original."

Alice scanned the page. "Angeline and Geoffrey?"

"Angeline was Mary Beth's great-great-grandmother, but Geoffrey wasn't her great-great-grandfather. We think he was the one who signed her dance card in 1861—the dance card she kept all her life. He had to have meant something to her."

"And he sent her this clue to something: 'A letter

brought you here and now you must find more.' What other letters was she supposed to find?"

"I guess that's what the clue will tell us."

"Hmmm." Alice leaned down, her elbows on the table, her forehead wrinkled. "They use the metric system in England, don't they? How many centimeters is forty-five inches?"

"Don't forget this is from 1861 or so. I don't think England used the metric system until about a hundred years later."

"OK, then what *did* they use for forty-five inches back then, smarty?"

"We'll come back to that one. What about the next clue? 'Twice indebted.'"

Alice finally pulled out a chair and sat down. "Double indemnity?"

"I don't think that's the same thing. There are two other 'twice' clues in here besides this one. Indebted, beholden, obliged, they all mean kind of the same thing, but they're somewhat different."

"Didn't you and Mary Beth work any of this out at her place?"

"Not really. We looked at it, but as excited as she was about this, Mary Beth seemed like she was really tired. I told her she should sleep on it and that I'd let you have a look too. Between the three of us, I'm sure we can figure it out." Annie tapped her pencil on the page. "How about this one. 'Katherine at home.'"

"Do you suppose Katherine was a friend of Mary Beth's great-great grandmother?"

"Could have been. She's in here twice. 'At home' and 'to her friends.'"

Alice frowned, thinking. "Maybe she had a nickname. I mean, that's what you'd use at home or with friends, right?"

"That seems logical. A Katherine would be called what? Kate? Katie?"

"Kit, maybe. Or Kay."

"Slow down." Annie started jotting down names next to the clue. "Kate, Katie, Kit, Kay. Maybe Kitty? Any others?"

"I'll keep thinking, but at least we have a start." Alice went over to the coffeemaker and filled both cups. "Where's your sugar?"

"Oh—I left it by the stove."

Alice added sugar and cream to both cups and brought them back to the table. "Did you and Mary Beth talk about anything?"

"You mean did we talk about her business problems? Not really. She pretty much cut me off when I tried to get the conversation turned that way."

"That means there *is* something going on with her. I wish she'd just tell us."

Annie took a sip of her coffee. "It's really not our business, you know, but I do want to help. I just wish I knew what else to do."

"You know, Annie, maybe we should put the puzzle up and do some brainstorming on how to help Mary Beth. Whatever these letters are that we're supposed to find, if they're even still around somewhere, they're not very likely to be a practical help to her."

"I suppose you're right." With a wistful sigh, Annie folded up her copy of the clue and put it in her purse. Then she pulled out a second notepad. "OK, let's brainstorm."

Alice and Annie spent the rest of the evening dreaming up and then discarding ideas until Alice finally gave up and went home to bed.

*   *   *   *

The next morning, Annie sat on the porch drinking coffee, watching the world wake up, and watching the sea. There was something mesmerizing about the waves that rushed to the shore, hurrying one after another only to immediately retreat. Annie listened to the hypnotic sound of the water as it crashed over and over against the rocks and sand, until the sound seemed to be a part of her, like the beating of her heart. Her gaze took in the gulls that circled endlessly above the water, which was gilded with the light of the dawn. The electronic ring of the telephone broke the spell.

"Hi Grammy!" called a chipper little voice as soon as she said hello. Her grandson—her little chip off the block—had always been an early riser, much to his mother's dismay.

"Hi there! How's my John?"

"We went swimming and rode a pony."

Annie smiled, picturing John's little face, big eyes shining, wiggling all over with excitement. "And when was this?"

"Yesterday. It was Mikey Morgan's birthday. He had a bounce house too. And I won some gummy worms for pinning the tail on the donkey."

"Oh, how fun. And did you have cake?"

"Uh-huh. It looked like a fire truck, but Jenny stuck her hand in it. Right where the ladder was."

Annie held back a giggle. "Oh, that's too bad. And who's Jenny?"

"Mikey's baby sister. He has two, but she's the little one. His other one is Kendra. Jenny just turned one year old."

"And did your sister go to the party too?"

"For a little while, but then she went home."

"That's not much like Joanna. Wasn't she having fun?"

"Until the clown came."

"Oh, dear. I know she doesn't like those. Was she OK?"

"She ran into the house and told Mommy she wanted to go home right then. But she didn't cry this time. Mommy said she was doing better."

"What did you think of the clown?"

"He smelled funny. Mommy said it probably was the kind of makeup he used. He made balloon animals, and those were cool, but besides that he was pretty lame."

Annie turned a laugh into a slight cough, wondering which of the "big kids" her grandson picked up his newest slang words from. "That's too bad. But I'm glad the party wasn't lame."

"Mom said when you come back home, and we have my birthday, we can have a pony again too."

"Well, that'll be fun."

"When are you coming home, Grammy? I mean *really* coming home and not just visiting?"

"Now, sweetie, you know I live up here now. My Grandma Betsy loved this house, and now I'm loving it for her too. You don't think she'd want me to let somebody else live in her house, do you?"

"No, I guess not," John said grudgingly. "Did she want you to leave us forever?"

"Now, honey, you know I haven't left you forever. I come see you all the time, don't I?"

"But you don't *live* here close to us like you used to. Mommy says it's like losing Grandpa all over again."

Annie felt a pain deep in her heart. After her husband Wayne's sudden death, her daughter LeeAnn had told her in so many words that she wasn't needed to help with the children anymore. Coming from Texas to Maine to see to Gram's estate had been a wonderful distraction, a chance to get away and establish herself as her own person, not just someone's mother or someone's grandmother. Now she was at home here in Stony Point, even though she knew LeeAnn and the kids would love to have her back.

"Sweetie," she said softly, "can you ask Mommy to come to the telephone?"

"Mooooooooooom! It's Grammy!"

Annie held the phone away from her ear until she heard her daughter's voice.

"Mom. Hi."

LeeAnn's voice sounded thick, a little sleepy. She hadn't been up long.

"I'm sorry, honey. I wasn't thinking about the time when I asked John to speak with you. I sometimes forget it's an hour earlier down there than it is up here. I didn't wake you, did I?"

"No, it's all right. I have to get going this morning anyway. I just hope John didn't wake *you* up. I've told him a hundred times—"

"No, no," Annie assured her, laughing. "You know me. I'm usually up with the sun."

"Yeah," LeeAnn deadpanned. "I remember."

"You're like your daddy. Some mornings he had to be pried out of bed."

"But he'd stay up half the night and watch movies with me." LeeAnn sighed. "I sure miss him."

Annie felt her throat tighten. Did it ever get any easier?

"I know you miss him, honey. I do too."

For a moment, there was only silence on the line. Then LeeAnn cleared her throat.

"So, how are you?"

"I'm all right, LeeAnn. I'm a little concerned about the kids."

"Really? Why?"

"John was asking me about coming back there for his birthday, and of course, I will. But I get the feeling he's upset because it will be just a visit."

"Well, I guess we're all getting used to you living up there now."

"Before I came up here, you told me you didn't need me anymore, didn't you?"

"I just meant you shouldn't feel tied down. I didn't mean we didn't want you." Again there were sudden tears in LeeAnn's voice. "And I didn't mean I didn't need you."

"I know, honey. Anyway, what's so bad about having a place that you and Herb and the kids can come visit when it's a hundred and ten in the shade down there in Texas?"

LeeAnn laughed. "Nothing at all."

"Now, you have to let me tell you about this key I found up in the attic."

"Oh Mom!" LeeAnn half scolded, half teased. "Another mystery?"

— 4 —

little before eleven, Annie hurried into A Stitch in Time, glad to see she was the only customer in the shop so far.

"Hi, Mary Beth. I know I'm a tiny bit early for the meeting, but I was hoping you had some new crochet patterns in. Does Kate have any new originals out? Where is she? Organizing your stock again?"

Mary Beth didn't quite look at her. "She's not working today, but she'll be here for the meeting."

Annie stepped lightly past the topic of Kate's reduced hours. "Oh, OK. Anyway ... I feel like making something really big this time, and I want to make an heirloom. How much of that glorious Two Ewe yarn do you have in stock?"

Mary Beth shook her head, and Annie could see now that her eyes were red-rimmed. "You don't have to do it anymore."

"What do you mean?"

"You and the rest of the club, you don't have to keep buying a lot of expensive stuff you don't really need. I know you mean well, and it means a lot to me that you're willing to do it, but you shouldn't."

"Mary Beth—"

"It's no use throwing good money after bad."

"What do you mean?"

Mary Beth managed half of a smile. "I mean I love you

all, more than I can say, but there's no reason for you to bankrupt yourselves trying to help me."

The bell on the front door jingled as Alice and Peggy came into the shop.

"Hi, girls." Peggy's bright expression faded. "What's going on?"

"Nothing's going on." Mary Beth gestured toward the circle of comfortable chairs that was home to the Hook and Needle Club, all business. "Make yourselves comfortable. Did you finish cross-stitching those Christmas ornaments yet, Alice?"

Alice glanced at Annie who could only shrug.

"Not quite, Mary Beth. I think I want to add some beading to them, just for the sparkle."

Mary Beth and Alice were looking over the bead rack when Kate and Gwen came in, followed by Stella, and they all settled into the sewing circle. Once Alice had made her selection, she joined them. Only Mary Beth was left standing, looking expectantly at them until their chatter died down.

"I'm glad everybody is here today. There are some things I need to let you all know."

Everyone looked at everyone else, worry in their eyes, but nobody said anything. Kate kept her head down, and there was an extra touch of color in her cheeks. Had Mary Beth decided to let her go all together?

"As I told Kate yesterday, my landlord, the owner of this building, has given me notice that he wants to sell out when my lease expires at the end of next month. He says he has a good offer for the place, but he wants to give me the chance to match it, if I'd like to stay."

Still no one said anything. Annie finally asked Mary Beth what they all wanted to know.

"What are you going to do?"

Mary Beth smiled wryly. "There's not much I *can* do. I don't have the money to buy him out. I'd have to have enough for the shop and the theater next door too. He has to sell both places. It doesn't matter anyway. My credit is already maxed out. I think I'm going to have to close up."

"Close up?" Peggy wailed. "You can't just close up. How will you live?"

"I'll just have to find a job, won't I?" Mary Beth shrugged. "Or maybe I'll retire."

"You're too young to retire," Stella said firmly. "Maybe in another twenty years, when you're my age. And who knows what's going to happen to Social Security anyway?"

"Do you know who he plans to sell to?" Gwen asked.

Mary Beth's mouth was tight. "They want to tear down this building and the theater to build a Burly Boy's Burger Barn, complete with drive-through, all-night service, searchlights, and a twenty-foot-tall Burly Boy looming over it. I think A Stitch in Time will mostly end up as the parking lot."

A chorus of groans went up from the members of the Hook and Needle Club.

"Not a Burly Boy!" Peggy moaned. "Not in Stony Point. What's that going to do to business at The Cup & Saucer?"

"What's it going to do to our quaint little village?" Annie pressed her lips together. "I can't believe the town council would allow that. Ian would never even consider such a thing."

"My guess is that Burly Boy made it well worth their while to reconsider some of the zoning restrictions." Mary Beth's smile was wry. "I guess our town is a little strapped for cash too."

"Then we just can't let it happen," Alice said. "We'll all chip in and help you keep the shop."

"We want to help," Gwen said when Mary Beth started to protest. "After all, we all love A Stitch in Time too."

Mary Beth squeezed her arm. "That's sweet, but it's not your problem. It's mine."

"But we can help, Mary Beth," Peggy insisted. "We already—" She broke off, eyes wide.

Mary Beth looked at her and then at the rest of the group. "Yes, Kate told me what you were already doing."

"We were just going to see if we could raise some money," Annie admitted when no one else spoke up. "It was supposed to be a surprise."

Peggy cringed. "Sorry."

"All we did was gather up some stuff to sell," Alice said. "It's not a big deal."

"Not a big deal?" Mary Beth shook her head. "You all amaze me. Thank you all for trying to help, but it's really something I'll have to figure out for myself."

"We've been worried about you," Alice told her. "We could tell you haven't been yourself lately."

"We didn't want you to lose the shop," Kate admitted, her head down and her dark hair falling to one side, concealing her face. "We just … . We wanted to do something to help you."

Annie took Mary Beth's hand, pulling her down into

the empty chair next to hers. "We're your best friends, Mary Beth. We know when something's wrong."

Mary Beth looked up at the ceiling, her eyes blinking rapidly. "You're not supposed to make me do this."

Peggy handed her a tissue. "There's nothing better than a good cry, I always say."

A quick dab of the tissue was all Mary Beth would allow herself. Then she straightened in her chair and put on a determined smile. "I love you all, really, but this isn't the end of the world. I'm a big girl, and this is *my* problem to work out. All I can do is work hard and pray hard and see what happens. You haven't sold any of your stuff yet, have you?"

Annie shook her head. "We've just been gathering things up."

"Well," Mary Beth said, emphatically, "then you ungather all of it. I mean it. I'm not going to have all of you giving up your nice things just because I hit a rough spot in the road."

"We can at least help you figure out what to do," Alice said. "I could always get you on at Divine Décor if you want me to."

"I don't know," said Mary Beth. "I'm comfortable with people I meet here in the familiar surroundings of my own shop, but I don't know if I could do what you do, Alice. Going to a different place for each customer's 'party' would seem like starting a new job each time. I suppose I could get used to it, if I had to."

Alice smiled. "I know what you mean," she said. "I felt the same way for a while when I started out, but you *do* get used to it, and the people who host these sort of parties are so nice."

"Or maybe you can move the shop," Gwen suggested. "If you found a cheaper place, maybe things wouldn't be quite so tight."

Mary Beth sighed. "I wish it were that easy. Besides, I don't think I could find a cheaper place. Not here in Stony Point. Mr. Huggins has been great about not raising my rent. He says getting paid regularly and on time is raise enough for him."

"I'm surprised by Jeb Huggins selling out this way," Stella said. "He's had this place for years now."

Mary Beth sighed. "That's the worst part. His wife has heart problems, and he's got to have money for all her medical expenses. No—I just have to face facts. Unless something happens, and that does *not* mean all of you bankrupting yourselves buying things here that you don't really need, then I'll have to close up."

Stella reached over and squeezed her hand. "I wish there was something I could do, dear. Mr. Brickson left me fairly well off, but most of what I have is in annuities and trusts. I couldn't lay my hands on enough cash at one time to really make much difference at this point."

"When do you have to give Mr. Huggins your answer?" Alice asked.

"I have till the end of next month to let him know."

"I thought you had some money put aside for times like this," Gwen said. "I know my husband advises you at the bank—not that he gives me details about any of his clients of course."

"I guess I should have listened to him when he told me to make safe, long-term investments. But I had a 'sure thing' awhile back and lost quite a bit of my savings. Now here I am."

"I was afraid that was what happened," Kate said. "I'm so sorry, Mary Beth. And I'm sorry for being such a blabbermouth."

"You're not a blabbermouth." Mary Beth reached across the circle to squeeze Kate's hand. "And thank you for worrying about me. Thanks, all of you, but you can stop now. I'll be fine. God knows what He's doing. If He wants me here, then He'll show me that. If not, I just have to believe He has something new for me to do. Now let's all get to work, or I'll have to change our name from the Hook and Needle Club to the 'Everybody Worry About Mary Beth Club.'"

Y   Y   Y   Y

"We're not really going to forget about helping Mary Beth, are we?" Alice asked as she and Annie walked back to their cars after the meeting was over.

"Of course we're not. And we're also not going to let this Burly Boy thing ruin the atmosphere of downtown Stony Point. I can't believe Ian would let that happen."

"There's big money behind that franchise, money Stony Point could use for a lot of good things."

Annie stopped in her tracks. "You're not saying you're behind this, are you?"

"Of course not. But nothing has happened yet. All we have to do is figure out how to keep A Stitch in Time right where it is, and there won't be any Burly Boy."

"I suppose you're right." Annie scowled. "That doesn't

make me any happier with our local government."

Alice laughed. "Just remember, they have tough decisions to make too. Don't snap Ian's head off next time you see him."

"Somebody mention my name?"

Alice and Annie both turned. Ian was leaning his tall, rugged frame against a lamp post, his smile crinkling the corners of his dark brown eyes.

Annie had to press her lips together hard to keep from doing just what Alice had warned her against.

"Hello, Ian," Alice said. "How's the lumber mill these days?"

He winced just a little. "Staying afloat."

"I guess times are hard for everybody," Annie said coolly. "Obviously you know about Mr. Huggins having to sell the Bijou Theater and the building that houses A Stitch in Time."

Ian straightened away from the lamp post. "I do, in fact. It's part of my job."

Feeling the heat rise in her face, Annie put her hands on her hips. "Is it also part of your job, Mr. Mayor, to sell out Stony Point to the highest bidder?"

Ian smiled and put his hands up, warding her off. "Whoa there. I'm the mayor, not the town council. There's only so much I can do on my own."

"But a Burly Boy? Really, Ian?"

"Don't be so upset, Annie. It's not a done deal yet. Not by a longshot."

"That's what I told her," Alice put in.

"I'm just sorry to hear Mary Beth is having a bad time," Ian said. "If she could stay in her building, then Burly Boy would have to go somewhere else. Huggins is the only one on the square willing to sell, and that's only because of his wife. And Burly Boy isn't interested in anything that's not right in the middle of town."

"But the zoning laws should be able to keep them out," Annie said, finding it harder and harder to be upset with the always-reasonable Ian.

"Not if the council finds that it's in the city's best interest to waive certain provisions," Ian explained. "The planning and zoning committee is looking into rezoning. If they make a recommendation to the council to rezone the property, there will have to be a public hearing. I'm sure there will be a lot of opposition, so—as I said—this is far from being a done deal. *Really*, Annie, I tried. I don't like it any better than you do."

Great. Now she was starting to feel sorry for him. Her expression softened. "I know you don't. And I'm sorry I snapped at you. I just hate to see anything happen to Stony Point. It's—well, it just means a lot to me."

He winked at her. "Come on, ladies. Since we can't get a Double Chili-Cheese Burly Boy Bonus Burger with Burly Fries here in town, I'll treat you both to a sandwich at The Cup & Saucer."

Annie and Alice smiled at each other, and then Alice took Ian's arm.

"You've got a date."

Ian held his other arm out invitingly. "Annie?"

Refusing to acknowledge Alice's insinuating smirk, Annie accepted. Arm in arm, the three of them walked over to The Cup & Saucer.

* * * *

With all the members of the Hook and Needle Club gone, Mary Beth took a moment to tidy up the shop. How could she stay down when so many people obviously cared about her and were praying for her?

She had just straightened out the display of hand-dyed embroidery floss when the phone rang.

"A Stitch in Time. This is Mary Beth. How can I help you?"

"Auntie Beth?"

Mary Beth smiled to hear Amy's voice over the telephone. "Well hello, sweetie. How are you?"

"I'm fine, but I wanted to find out how you are."

"I'm doing all right." Mary Beth sank down into one of the shop's comfy chairs. "How's your mom? Have you heard from her lately?"

"Oh, you know how it is." Amy's voice took on the indifferent tone that she usually used when she talked about her mother, Melanie. "She's in Milan or something. I don't know."

"I'm sure she'll give you a call when she gets back."

"Yeah, I guess."

Poor Amy. As much as she tried, Mary Beth could never seem to make up for Melanie's maternal shortcomings.

"I wish you two were closer, honey. I know your mother would like that."

Amy sighed. "I'll give her a call as soon as I find out where she is—if she's not too busy to talk, OK?"

"That'd be great."

"Anyway, I didn't call to talk about her. I called to talk about you. I've been worried about you."

"Me? Why would you worry about me?"

"I don't know. You've seemed ... distracted the last couple of times I've talked to you. Is everything all right?"

"Nothing you need to worry about. Really. It's just that Mr. Huggins may be selling this building, and that means I'm going to have to make some changes."

"Oh Auntie Beth, no. Does that mean you have to move the shop? Can't you just keep renting from the new owner?"

"It's not as easy as that," Mary Beth admitted. "The buyer they're considering wants to tear down my place and the theater next door to put in a fast-food restaurant."

"That's just not right. Can't *you* buy the building?"

Mary Beth laughed. It was easier than crying. "You know I don't have that kind of money, sweetie."

"Maybe I could—"

"No, you're not going to do anything silly. I know how hard you've worked for what you have, and I know things haven't been easy for you lately either. I'll be fine. Really. Things will work out."

Amy was silent for a long moment. "But you love the shop. And you've worked hard for it too. It's not right for you to lose it after all these years."

"I don't know that there's any right and wrong about it. Businesses either make it, or they don't. No matter how hard you try, sometimes you have to try something else. But I'm not giving up quite yet, sweetie. We'll see what happens. Either way, I don't want you to worry about me. I'd rather tell you about something exciting that happened.

Annie Dawson was up in her grandmother's attic the other day. You remember all the stuff she has up there. Turns out your grandmother had given Annie's grandmother a little china vase on a brass stand … ."

— 5 —

Once Mary Beth had told Amy about the key and the table and the clue Geoffrey Whyte had left for Angeline to find, she found her mood had improved, and Amy didn't sound quite as anxious as she had when she first called. By the time she told her niece goodbye, she was humming and tidying up the shop. She felt particularly cheery when the phone rang again.

"A Stitch in Time. This is Mary Beth. How can I help you?"

"Um, hi. Miss Brock? This is Mandy Culbertson. I wanted to know if today was a good day for me to come and help you at your store."

"Oh."

Mary Beth blinked, hardly knowing what to say in response. She had totally forgotten about agreeing to let Amanda work at the shop. It had seemed like a good idea at the time to her and to Amanda's mother when they had discussed it after the accident. After all, the girl should take some responsibility for the damage her carelessness had caused. Now Mary Beth wasn't sure she felt like dealing with it.

"Um ... yes, hi, Mandy. How are you?"

"I'm fine. I just got caught up on some research I had to do for a school paper, so I thought I'd come by and help you for a while."

"Uh … yeah. OK. Umm, you know, Mandy, I appreciate your wanting to help and everything, and I was very happy to have you help getting the glass all cleaned up and the merchandise put back where it belonged after the accident, but really, that was plenty. I don't think you need to—"

"But, Miss Brock, I *really* want to help. I know the insurance paid for everything, but that accident was totally my fault, and I want to make it up to you. Please."

"That *is* very sweet of you, Mandy." Mary Beth looked around trying to figure out what the girl could do that would be helpful and not need constant supervision. "Um, when would you like to come?"

"Whenever you want. I can come now, if you want me to. Is that all right?"

"Um, sure. Right now is good." *Except I don't have a clue what to do with you when you get here.* "That'll be great, Mandy. I'll see you in a little while."

A few minutes later, as she was tidying up a display of new yarns at the back of the shop, Mary Beth heard the front door open. Mary Beth quickly stuffed the yarns in the appropriate basket and called out, "Hi, Mandy—that was quick! You must have been just down the street."

Mary Beth walked to the front of the shop, expecting to see the teenage girl, but instead, an imposing-looking, thirty-something woman and a very young man stood just inside the front door. It wasn't Mandy Culbertson. It wasn't anyone she'd ever seen before.

"Ms. Brock?" said the woman.

Mary Beth's face had registered her surprise, but then she put on a pleasant, professional smile. "I'm sorry. I was expecting someone else. But, yes, I'm Mary Beth Brock. What can I do for you?"

The woman snapped her manicured fingers, and the baby-faced young man behind her handed her a business card. She immediately thrust the card at Mary Beth.

"I'm Kyrie McMillan. I'm with SLR & FFH, Incorporated. You know us better as Burly Boy's Burger Barns. As you may know, we're in the process of purchasing this property for development. With your permission, we'd like to do a brief review of the interior, including the basement and any access areas, in order to get a better idea not only of an appropriate purchase price, but also any potential assets or materials that could be salvaged before demolition of the building."

"Whoa, whoa, whoa. What was that?"

The woman looked as if she wanted to roll her eyes. "With your permission, we'd like to do a brief review of the interior, including the basement and any access areas—"

"I got that part. What I didn't get is that you had actually made a deal to buy this property or that Mr. Huggins had given you permission to, what did you say? 'Review the interior'?"

The woman's young assistant squirmed in his too-large suit coat, but he didn't make a sound. The woman, on the other hand, did not look as if she were one to squirm at all. Ever.

"I understand the final details are being worked out with the owner, Mr. ..."

She turned to glare at her assistant who was fumbling with some papers in a file folder.

"Mr. Huggins," he whispered.

"Mr. Huggins." The woman turned again to Mary Beth. "But, as you can well understand, Ms. Brock, it's helpful to do a certain amount of planning even before the actual deal is agreed upon. I trust you have no objections to us merely looking at the property? We promise not to disturb anything or interfere with your customers." She peered into the shop. "If any should actually come in."

Mary Beth managed to keep smiling. "I think, seeing as you don't actually have a contract in place for this property, I would rather wait until Mr. Huggins—"

"Get Huggins on the phone," the woman directed her assistant. "He'll be at that medical center number in the file."

He took a phone from his inside pocket and started punching in numbers. Obviously, neither of them cared that Mr. Huggins was at the hospital with his ailing wife.

"No, wait." Mary Beth exhaled heavily. "Don't bother him now. If you really think you need to, come on in and look around all you like."

The young man secreted the phone in his inside pocket once more, and Mary Beth stepped aside to let him and his boss into the shop.

"The back room is through there, and you'll find the steps to the basement in there too. Still, I hate to see you wasting your time here if Mr. Huggins doesn't end up selling to you."

The other woman smirked. "That won't happen, Ms. Brock. I've been handling these demos for a lot of years. Some of the owners and residents squawk a little at first, especially in the smaller towns, but they finally come around. There's no stopping progress. Come along, Greg."

The two of them disappeared into the back room. A few minutes later, they were back up again, the young assistant writing down his boss's observations as quickly as she could fire them off.

"Is that all?" Mary Beth asked when the woman appeared to be slowing down.

"For now. That shelving in your basement. It looks relatively new."

"It is."

"Good. If you'll have everything cleared out of it, we'll arrange to have it picked up right away."

"Picked up?"

"Yes. Picked up. Hauled off. No use having it bulldozed with everything else. It looks in good shape. It ought to bring a little money."

"Ms. ..." Mary Beth looked at the business card she still held. "Ms. McMillan, those are *my* shelves. I put them down there. If you do end up buying the building—and that's not nearly a settled fact yet—my shelves won't have anything to do with your deal with Mr. Huggins."

"Our standard contract specifies that purchase of the property includes anything attached to the building. That would, of course, include any built-in additions."

Mary Beth managed to keep her tone of voice low and pleasant. "That may well be the case, but for one thing, those shelves aren't built in. I ordered them to fit that space, but they're not attached. For another thing, your standard contract isn't applicable until and unless Mr. Huggins signs it."

"As you say." The woman took a pair of designer sunglasses out of her purse and put them on. "That being the case, if you're planning to take them with you, it will save you some time and trouble later on if you go ahead and pack up whatever is in those cabinets, your merchandise, I presume, and clear them out now. I understand Huggins wants to make a quick deal, and so do we. Good afternoon, Ms. Brock. Greg."

Greg mumbled a quick goodbye and trotted after her through the door.

For a moment, Mary Beth could only stare after them. Then she turned away from the door and looked over the little shop that she had worked so hard to make appealing to people like herself—people who loved all kinds of needlework.

"And just how am I supposed to keep my customers happy if all my merchandise is packed up in storage? Oh, that's right, I don't *have* any customers. Thank you very much, Ms. Whoever-You-Are." She glanced again at the business card. All it had under the SLR & FFH, Incorporated logo was "Kyrie McMillan, Corporate Planning," an email address and six different telephone numbers. "Ms. Corporate Planner then. Fine. We'll see whether or not you always get your way."

"What'd you say, Miss Brock?"

Mary Beth started and turned around to see Amanda Culbertson had slipped inside without her noticing. She laughed and said, "Mandy! Where'd you come from?"

"I was just over at the library. I had a little free time, and it seemed like a good opportunity to come help you out. Who were those people who just left your shop? I've never seen them around town."

Mary Beth pursed her lips as she watched their black SUV hurry down Main Street. "Well, I hope we won't see them much more. If at all." Abruptly, she smiled and ushered

Mandy into the shop. "Now how are you at alphabetizing?"

Amanda frowned, slightly puzzled. "OK, I guess."

"Good." Mary Beth took her to the wall of pattern books at the back of the store. "Sometimes customers don't put things back in the right places, and I don't always notice. Could you go through all these books and make sure they're in the right category—crochet, knitting, sewing, etc.—and then alphabetize according to the last name of the author?"

"Sure. That's easy enough."

"And if the same author wrote more than one book, then put the titles for that author in alphabetical order too—OK?"

"Got it."

"Thank you, Mandy. You're going to be a great help."

Mary Beth's smile faded when the girl's hot-pink cellphone suddenly blared out a rap tune with unintelligible lyrics and something that sounded like car crashes in the background. Cringing, Amanda glanced at the caller ID and then turned the phone off.

"Sorry about that, Miss Brock. They can leave a message."

Mary Beth's smile returned. "That's very considerate. Thank you."

Seeing that Mandy was going to be busy for a while, Mary Beth went into the back room and ate the tuna sandwich and potato chips she had brought from home. When she came back into the front of the store, she was surprised to see Ian Butler coming through the front door.

"Ian. Hi. Did you decide to take up knitting?"

Ian laughed, his dark eyes warm. "Actually, I came to talk to you, if you have a minute."

"Sure. It's been Grand Central Station around here this morning. But Mandy is tidying up my books for me, so at the moment, I'm a lady of leisure. Come sit down."

She led him to the circle of chairs usually occupied by the ladies of the Hook and Needle Club, and both of them had a seat.

"So what's on your mind, Ian?"

"I just had lunch with Annie and Alice. They're about ready to make war on the town council over this thing with Burly Boy."

"Ugh. Don't even mention that name to me right now. I just got a visit from somebody in Corporate Planning or something."

"Was it that McMillan woman?"

"I take it you've already met her."

Ian shuddered. "I was just glad it wasn't in a dark alley."

"She's not that bad," Mary Beth said, chuckling. "She's just very used to getting her own way."

"Was that her in the SUV?"

Mary Beth nodded. "And her little assistant, the poor thing—he looked all of twelve years old."

"Poor kid. What did they want?"

"They were scouting out the place, acting as if it already belonged to SPQR & FFA, Incorporated—or whatever it is. I couldn't believe it, Ian."

"You should have told them to come back when they have a contract."

Mary Beth shrugged. "I did, more or less, but then she was going to call up Mr. Huggins at the hospital to get his OK, and I really didn't want them bothering him right now, you know? Not with his wife as sick as she is."

"I can understand that." He gave her a rueful, sympathetic smile. "They didn't stay long, did they?"

"Just long enough to ruffle my feathers, and that was way too long."

"I'll try extra hard to stay on your good side then. I don't think I could take another beating like the one I got over lunch."

"From Annie and Alice?" Mary Beth held up one hand. "I *swear*, Ian, I didn't send them over to see you."

Ian chuckled. "I know, but I couldn't blame you if you had. I'm none too happy about the deal either. But there's something else I hope you'll understand about why we're not trying to stop the sale to Burly Boy. Mr. Huggins needs that money. We'd rather he sold the place to you or to some other investor who would let you keep your store. But he needs to sell, and if Burly Boy is his only option, it'd be pretty heartless for us to stop him and keep his wife from getting the care she needs, wouldn't it?"

"Nobody wants that. And I hope it doesn't come to that. I don't want the town council to miss out on anything that would actually be good for Stony Point in the long run either."

"Obviously, we want to keep the character of our downtown. Stony Point should stay looking like Stony Point and not Las Vegas or New York, right?"

Mary Beth chuckled. "Right."

"But there are purely financial considerations also. Not only are the Burly Boy people willing to pay well for the privilege of opening on our Main Street, they'd bring in some good sales tax revenues for years to come as well as provide some entry-level and even management jobs that we desperately need."

She felt bad for Ian. Life was hard enough these days. He and the town council had not only themselves to consider, but also the welfare of the whole town. Keeping Stony Point's traditions and way of life alive while not killing its industry and growth had to be a delicate balancing act.

"I can see how that would be a hard decision, especially with Mr. Huggins in his situation. Maybe keeping my little shop open isn't the best thing for the town."

"No, no, that's not what I mean at all. I'm just saying we all have some hard decisions to make. The way I see it, Mr. Huggins would rather sell to you than anyone. We all want you to stay in Stony Point. If you can figure out how to pull that off, then it's a no-brainer. You stay, everybody's happy. But if you can't, there's not much more for us to do than to let Mr. Huggins get his money however he can and make the best of it for Stony Point."

"I wish I knew what was going to happen, Ian. Right now, I'm just praying hard and keeping my eyes open."

"I guess that's the best thing any of us can do right now." He stood up and gave her shoulder a pat. "If there's anything I can do for you, Mary Beth, you let me know."

"I will." She followed him to the front door. "Um, you will let me know before there's anything final about the sale, won't you?"

"I thought Mr. Huggins was holding off until the end of next month."

"Oh, he is. But I know he's got a pretty hard situation to deal with, and if the Burly Boy people put more pressure on him, he might change his mind. I couldn't really blame him."

"But he'd have to have approval first from the planning and zoning commission and the council before that kind of deal could go through," Ian reminded her.

"I know. So I figure you'll know about it if anything changes."

His eyes crinkled at the corners. "All right. If I hear any news like that, I'll let you know. Meanwhile, you keep those eyes open."

"I will."

Again he patted her shoulder. "And don't worry—OK?"

"Thanks."

She shut the front door after him and turned around to find Mandy right behind her.

"Oh!"

"Sorry. I didn't mean to scare you, Miss Brock. I'm done though, and I thought you'd want to take a look."

Mary Beth forced a smile, not sure what her book wull would look like now, but the smile soon widened into a genuine grin.

"That looks great, Mandy. Everything is so neat and well organized."

Mandy fairly beamed under the praise. "Thanks. I hope I did it all right."

Mary Beth wrapped one arm around the girl's shoulders. "You did it perfectly. Now, if you still want to help, I've been wanting to reorganize my patterns too. I think between the two of us, we can just get it done before closing time. Can you stay that long?"

"Sure. Just let me call my mom and let her know."

While Mandy was calling home, Mary Beth was surprised to see Kate come into the shop.

"Hi there!" Mary Beth hugged her. "I didn't expect you in today."

"I've been busy during my time off." Kate held up an overstuffed tote bag. "I've printed up a bunch of copies of my new patterns, and I was hoping you'd have room for them in the display."

"Oh, wonderful!" Mary Beth hugged her again, almost in tears. "Thank you for being so understanding about this whole mess, Kate. You don't know how much I miss having you in the shop every day. I hope it won't be long before I can bring you back full-time."

Kate gave her a hopeful little smile. "I was thinking about that. I've been busy working on patterns and packaging them for sale. I thought—if you don't object, that is—I could do that here as easily as at home. Then I could help out with customers, too, if you needed me to. No wages required. What do you think?"

"Oh, Kate, really?"

Kate nodded eagerly.

"No, I couldn't." Mary Beth shook her head. "I couldn't take advantage of you like that."

"What advantage? I told you I'd be doing exactly what I'm doing at home right now. Only it's not nearly as fun doing it by myself and without someone to bounce ideas off of. You've always been such a help to me when I'm working up a new idea. What do you say?"

Mary Beth gave her an enormous hug. "Welcome back!"

—6—

The rest of the afternoon flew by, but Mary Beth was pleased with how neat and appealing the shop looked after a little straightening up, and she was thrilled to have Kate in the shop again. By the time she got home, her telephone was ringing. She tossed her purse into a chair and picked up the receiver.

"Hello?"

"You know, Mary Beth, I really don't appreciate you using Amy to try to manipulate me!"

"Melanie?"

"I know you've always felt like I had it easier than you, but I've worked for everything I have. I took chances to make it big instead of being satisfied with a one-off little craft store in a town nobody ever heard of. Now you think *I'm* the one who has to bail *you* out? You could have gotten into the business when I did. Mother would've found a place for you somewhere, I guess. But you had to waltz over to Hickville in the backwoods and be on your own. Well, this is the 'on your own' part, sister."

"Well, how nice to hear from you, Melanie. How have you been?"

"Don't be cute. You're not the type. And I don't appreciate what you're trying to do."

Mary Beth clamped her jaws so tightly shut she was

surprised they didn't creak, but she was not going to give her sister the fight she was obviously looking for. She merely counted to ten.

"Mary Beth? Are you listening to me?"

Mary Beth let her breath out slowly and forced a smile that she hoped would show in her voice. "Of course I'm listening, Melanie. I just don't know what you're talking about." She sank down into the chair and then shifted to pull her forgotten purse out from under herself. "How about starting at the beginning and telling me what's going on?"

"Don't try that on me, Miss Innocent. I know you talked to Amy today."

"Yes, I did. She is my niece, you know."

"That doesn't mean you can use her to do your dirty work, Mary Beth."

"What's that supposed to mean?"

"She asked me to make you a loan. Don't tell me you didn't put her up to that."

Mary Beth leaned her head back and closed her eyes. "Think whatever you want to, but I didn't. I don't know why you'd think that. I don't think she'd even say I'd do some-thing like that."

"She told me it was all her idea, but don't think for a minute I don't know you didn't call her up to complain about how bad things are for you. But—with the Lord's help, of course—you'll make it through somehow."

Her sister's voice had turned into a mocking imitation of a pathetic whine, and for some strange reason, in a bad southern accent on top of it all. Again, Mary Beth had to count to ten.

"Look, Melanie," she said finally, "Amy is a sweet girl, and it's good of her to be concerned about me, but I would never ask her for anything. I certainly wouldn't ask her to ask *you* for anything. And heaven knows, the last thing I would do is expect anything from you. I told her, and I'll tell you right now, honestly, sincerely, and with no misunderstandings and no hidden messages: I will work this out. I don't know what's going to happen, but I'll figure out something. And yes, with the Lord's help—thank you very much—I'll be fine."

Melanie only made an impatient little huffing sound.

"I know you don't understand me, Mel. You never did. Mother never did. The fashion business is just not important to me. I would hate living your life. I know you have the money and the fame. I know you go everywhere and know everyone who is anyone and are in all the fashion magazines. I'm glad you have what you want. Honestly, I am. But I could never live that way. I love Stony Point and A Stitch in Time. I love my little house and my ordinary friends and my quiet life. And I know you think it's just hysterically funny, but I do believe God will look after me and show me what I need to do when the time comes to close the shop. *If* the time comes."

"You tell yourself whatever you need to, Mary Beth. Whatever gets you by. But don't bring Amy into it! Do you understand?"

"I didn't bring her into it. In fact, I told her I absolutely did not want her to do anything. And believe it or not, I don't expect anything from you either. We're both grown up. We make our decisions, and we deal with what comes of them. I'm just sorry that you feel like I'm trying to manipulate you or Amy." Mary Beth swallowed hard. "And I'm sorry the only time we ever talk is when something is wrong."

The only answer she got was a click followed by a dial tone.

*   *   *   *

As soon as Annie and Alice had finished their lunch with Ian at The Cup & Saucer, Annie went on a fact-finding mission that took most of the afternoon. The minute she got home, she dropped in over at Alice's.

"Do you have time for company, Alice? You won't believe what I found."

Alice snorted. "You won't believe how many rivers they have in Scotland. That's one clue that's going to be hard to pin down. Come on in."

"Hmmm, so that's not going to help us get started." Annie followed Alice inside, and they both made themselves comfortable on the couch. "Any luck on any of the other clues?"

"Well, thanks to the Internet, I found out that an old English measurement that happens to be 45 inches is called an ell. I'm thinking 'Roadside Refuge' is an inn."

Annie dug out her copy of Geoffrey's clues. "OK, I guess we can pencil those in. Anything else?" She cleared her throat and read the paper aloud:

> "*England's 45 inches*
> *Twice indebted*
> *Katherine at home*

Blue and twinkling
Roadside refuge

Turn to the right
Twice beholden
Scotland's river

Busy sweets maker
Twice obliged
Katherine to her friends"

Alice wrinkled her forehead in thought. "'Blue and twinkling' I was thinking could be eyes or maybe just eye, but it doesn't make sense. Eye Inn? Do you suppose that was a tavern or something back then? Maybe that's where he hid the next letter Angeline was supposed to find."

Annie swatted herself on the forehead. "I can't believe I'm so stupid. The letters she was supposed to find aren't the kind you write *to* someone. They're the kind you write *with*. They're all right there. Not the words 'eye inn' but the letters 'IN.' That spells 'in'! Ell, the 45-inch unit of length in England, is for the letter L. 'Katherine to her friends' must be Kay, the letter K."

"Wait, wait! I'm trying to write these down. Then a 'busy sweets maker' has got to be a bee—the letter B." Alice giggled. "It's pretty easy when you know how."

Annie frowned at the piece of paper she held. "I don't know. What word starts with L and ends with K and has only three letters? The middle has to be a vowel, but none of them make this a real word. The same with the last three lines. B something K. It doesn't make sense."

"Sure it does. Think about it. 'Indebted,' 'beholden,' 'obliged' all mean the same thing, or the same letter. And the 'twice' just means that letter is used two times."

Annie went through the vowels in her head and suddenly laughed. "Of course. *Owe.* I can't believe I didn't get that right off. That just leaves us with 'turn to the right' and 'Scotland's river.'"

Alice went to her computer and clicked a few keys. "Well the only river I see that is also a letter would be the river Dee."

"Perfect." Annie penciled in the letter D. "Now, what do we have? 'LOOK IN _OOD BOOK.' There are only a few letters that would fit there and make a word: F, G, H, M, and W, and I don't think he would have had a 'hood book' or a 'mood book.'"

Alice snickered.

Annie tapped her pencil on the table, thinking. "So that leaves F, G, and W."

"A wood book?" Alice asked.

"Maybe, but F and W aren't words by themselves."

"And G is? I don't know. And what does it have to do with turning?"

Annie caught her breath. "No, no, that's it! Didn't you ever read the *Little House on the Prairie* books?"

"No, but I watched the TV show. Does that count?" Alice asked dubiously.

Annie laughed. "Maybe. What we keep forgetting to do is keep in mind when this clue was written: 1861 or so. They used to shout 'gee' and 'haw' as a voice command to oxen or horses to get them to pull right or left. I never could remember which was which, but going by this, 'gee' must have been right."

"'LOOK IN GOOD BOOK.' Umm. And what was his idea of a good book?"

"Alice! Not *a* good book, *the* Good Book—the Bible!"

"Oh, duh! That must be where the numbers come in. Let's see, there are four in each line. Umm ... book, chapter, verse and word?"

"We won't know till we try. Do you have one handy?"

"Yeah," Alice said, "hang on."

Alice disappeared into her bedroom and came back with her Bible.

"OK, the fiftieth book is ... Philippians."

"Right," Annie said. "Listen to make sure we're doing it right, let's both look these up and compare answers. Do you have another copy?"

"Sure. The old one my grandmother had. Let me get it."

They both flipped pages and made notes until Alice finally put down her Bible with a sigh.

"I think we have the wrong book, Annie. Or we have the wrong idea about what the numbers mean. It doesn't make sense."

Annie glanced over what she had so far. "Tell me what you've got."

"'Each in the table no the they secret and.' Something's wrong, or he's the worst clue writer ever."

"Alice—"

"I mean, who writes 'no the they'?"

"Alice, which Bible are you looking at?"

"The one I always use. The NIV."

"And how many copies of the New International Version of the Bible did they have in the 1860s?"

"Ohhhhh." Alice laughed. "OK, so what did you and your King James Version get, smarty?"

"'Look in the writing table in the deeper secret place.'"

"Yeah," Alice deadpanned, "now *that* makes much more sense."

"So it's a little odd, but it's better than 'no the they,' isn't it?"

"Hmm ... Did Mary Beth say her great-great-grand-mother had left her a writing table?"

"I don't remember," Annie admitted. "Maybe we'd better give her a call."

"First you have to tell me what you found out. You said something about it before we got distracted with solving this."

"Tell you what," Annie said, "why don't we go see Mary Beth? Then I can tell you both at the same time. I'm not sure how much help it will be at this point, but I think it's something Mary Beth will want to know."

"Great! We'll take the Mustang."

*   *   *   *

Alice's red Mustang had them at Mary Beth's house in record time. Annie had called Mary Beth on the way, and she was waiting for them when they pulled up in the driveway.

"Oh, hurry! I can't wait to hear the news."

"Which do you want first?" Alice asked, her blue eyes twinkling. "The answer to the puzzle, or what Annie found out about the guy who wrote it?"

"Oh, the puzzle." Mary Beth hurried them into her living room. "I've had so much going on, I haven't had a chance to really look at it."

They sat down, and Alice spread her copy of the clue on the table. "It was actually fairly simple. Each word sounds like a letter, and the letters spell out the clue: LOOK IN GOOD BOOK."

Mary Beth's eyes lit. "Then the numbers are all Bible references."

"Exactly," Annie said. "But only the King James Version."

Alice laughed. "It makes a difference. Trust me."

Mary Beth picked up the page, squinting at Annie's erased and rewritten words. "'Look in writing table in the deeper secret place'?"

Annie nodded. "Did your great-great-grandmother leave you a writing table or a desk of some kind?"

Mary Beth's face fell. "Yes. Oh Annie, she did."

Annie glanced at Alice, seeing the bewilderment on her friend's face. "Can we see it?"

"I sold it to Bob Kelsey last month."

7

"Sold it?"

Annie and Alice spoke at the same time, and Mary Beth could only nod, misery etched in every line of her face.

"Bob gave me a good price for it, and it was either that or have my lights and water cut off. Here and at the shop."

"Call him," Alice said, thrusting the telephone at her. "He can at least let you see if there's anything in the table."

Mary Beth looked at her for a moment and then grabbed her purse. "I kept his card," she said with a knowing grin, "in case I had something else I needed to sell."

They all waited, listening to the whirring of the phone ringing on the other end of the line. Finally there was a click. All three of them groaned to hear the recorded message: "You've reached Bob Kelsey at Kelsey's Odds and Ends. I'd love to talk antiques with you. Leave a message, and I'll get right back to you."

There was a beep.

"Bob, this is Mary Beth Brock. I need to talk to you right away about the writing desk I sold you last month. Please give me a call as soon as you can." She gave him her phone number and then repeated her name and number again. "Call me."

She exhaled loudly as she hung up. "I hope it's not too late. I mean, he may have already sold it to someone."

"It's OK, Mary Beth." Annie reached over and squeezed her hand. "If he did, he'll know who it was, and we can call them."

Mary Beth didn't seem convinced. "Sure."

"Do you think he'll call right back?" Alice looked at Mary Beth and then at Annie. "Maybe we could wait a few minutes and see if he does."

"Sure," said Annie. "If you don't mind, Mary Beth. In the meantime, I can tell you what I found out in my research."

Mary Beth nodded.

"I did verify that your great-great-grandmother Angeline Morrow was married to James Parish in 1866. It was pretty easy to trace down from them to you. Geoffrey was a little bit harder to find, but I finally did. He was born in Fairfax County, Virginia, in 1839. His family was fairly prominent at the time, very well off and well connected. But everything I found indicates that, by the end of the Civil War, the money was gone and so was the last of the family. His mother, Georgianna Flippin Whyte, was evidently a very strong woman. She ran the family plantation and the other businesses they owned. Her husband died several years before the war, and she put all her hopes into her only son, Geoffrey. He was killed in the first battle of Bull Run in 1861."

"Oh, how sad!" Mary Beth exclaimed.

"For his mother and for your great-great-grandmother, evidently," Alice added. "What happened to Georgianna?"

Annie shook her head. "I saw a copy of an obituary from November of 1865. It reported she had passed away 'after several months of decline.' Probably starved. Those were hard times in the South."

"Poor woman, and poor Angeline," Alice said. "You don't have anything else of hers that could have been from him, do you, Mary Beth?"

"I don't think so. There's a white rose in the back of her Bible pressed inside a folded sheet of paper. All it says is 'Easter Sunday 1861.' I've always wondered who it was from, and why she always kept it. I don't suppose we'll ever know for certain."

"How romantic," Alice breathed. "It must have been from the last time she ever saw him."

"*If* it was from him," Annie reminded her. "Maybe it was from another beau or from her father. Or maybe she picked it herself."

Alice scowled. "You're no fun."

"Anyway," Mary Beth said firmly, "whether the rose was from him or not, she must have gotten over his death. From all accounts, she and my great-great-grandfather were very happy together."

"You're no fun either," Alice grumbled. "How are we going to uncover a tragic romance if you both keep spoiling things?"

Just then Mary Beth's phone rang.

"Hello?"

Annie could hear the indistinct tones of a man's voice from where she sat. Mary Beth was nodding excitedly.

"Yes, Bob. Thanks for calling me back. I was wondering if I could come take a look at that writing desk I sold you. Just for a minute." Mary Beth paused, listening, and then her face fell. "I see. No, of course."

Annie and Alice exchanged glances. This couldn't be good.

"No," Mary Beth said after another pause. "I was just afraid I had left something important in it."

As the man replied, Mary Beth grabbed the pencil and pad of paper that was next to her phone. She jotted down a name and a phone number, and then smiled again.

"Thank you. I'll give them a call."

"Well?" Alice asked once she hung up. "What happened to the desk?"

Mary Beth sighed. "He sold it to another dealer in Portland with a lot of other pieces. They picked it up on Monday."

Annie frowned. "Can you call them?"

"Not until Monday now." Mary Beth folded the piece of paper with the phone number on it and slipped it into her purse. "Bob says they close at four o'clock weekdays and don't have any business hours on the weekends. It's probably one of those posh, by-appointment places."

Annie frowned, thinking. "OK, so we can't look at it tonight. What do you remember about the desk, Mary Beth. Did it have any hidden drawers or cubbyholes? Any secret places?"

"What did it look like anyway?" Alice asked.

There was a sudden wistfulness in Mary Beth's eyes. "It was really pretty, solid cherry with a little inlaid pattern of teak and ash around the edge. It had three drawers in the front, and on top it had another stack of drawers and slots, and little cabinets with doors on them. Wait a second."

She scurried out of the room and came back a few minutes later with a framed photograph in her hands.

"You can see some of it in this picture."

Alice took it from her. "Ooh, isn't that pretty?"

Annie looked over Alice's shoulder at the large black-and-white photograph. It showed a little more than half of the writing desk that looked just as Mary Beth had described it. In front of it, an old woman sat in a rocking chair holding a wide-eyed baby in a lace christening gown. The woman wore a high-necked black dress with a pearl brooch at the collar, and her snow-white hair was twisted into a bun at the back of her neck. Her expression was solemn, but there was something vivid about her eyes, which were dark and expressive, and something still lovely in the curve of her cheek. She must have been a beauty in her day.

"Is that her, Mary Beth?" Annie asked. "Is that Angeline?"

"As a matter of fact, it is. She was holding my mother a few weeks after she was born."

Annie smiled. "My goodness, how long ago was that?"

"It was 1922," Mary Beth said. "Angeline had just celebrated her eightieth birthday. Mom was her first great-grandchild."

"Amazing." Annie took the picture from Alice so she could take a closer look at the writing desk. "It looks like there are a lot of potential secret places in the desk."

"I gave it a pretty good going over before Bob picked it up. There is a little cubbyhole with a door on it behind that panel there." Mary Beth pointed to a place on the right side of the desk. "It has a keyhole, but I never saw a key for it. It wasn't locked anyway, and there wasn't anything in it."

Annie exhaled impatiently. "And we're back to the possibility that whatever Geoffrey left for Angeline might not be there anymore."

"If that's the place he meant," Mary Beth said, "then you're right. It's been empty at least since I was a little girl."

"I guess we could go ahead and see if the key we found with the clue fits it. If it does, we'll know that's where it was supposed to be."

"If Park Cambridge Antique Shoppe still has the desk on Monday." Mary Beth's shoulders sagged. "I could have used a little good news today. Now the best we can hope for is just knowing it's a dead end."

Annie glanced at Alice and then smiled at Mary Beth. "I know. Why don't we make a girls' day out of it? We can drive to Portland and look at the desk. We can have lunch somewhere fun and then do some shopping."

"Thanks, Annie, but I really can't—"

"Sure you can. You're closed on Mondays."

A little color came into Mary Beth's cheeks. "I don't want to spoil the fun, but I really can't afford a shopping spree right now."

"Come on," Annie coaxed. "We can just window-shop. That's still free. I'll drive, and lunch will be on me. You won't be out anything but a little time. What do you think?"

There was a little twitch at the corner of Mary Beth's mouth. "OK."

Annie clapped her hands together. "Great. Are you in, Alice?"

"Sorry, not for Monday. I have a Divine Décor party at eleven and then a Princessa jewelry party at three. Some of us have to work, you know."

Annie wrinkled her nose. "Now who's no fun?"

*   *   *   *

Monday turned out to be a beautiful day. It was a little bit cold for May, but the sky was a delicious clear blue, and spring was in its full riotous glory. Mary Beth was sitting on her front porch when Annie pulled up in her driveway, and she immediately scurried out to the car.

"Right on time," she said as she buckled herself in.

Annie smiled. "Of course. And don't you look nice. Did you make that?"

"Just finished it yesterday." Mary Beth fingered the lightweight ecru pullover she had crocheted. "It's one of Kate's patterns. She always lets me test them before she prints them up for sale."

"It's great. And just right for you."

Mary Beth chuckled. "I had been griping about how all the patterns are designed for girls in their twenties who look like fashion models. Kate's so sweet, I think she designed it especially to flatter someone with—ahem—a fuller figure."

Annie laughed with Mary Beth, happy to see she was in a more cheerful mood than she had been lately. Obviously Mary Beth was feeling better with Kate being back at the shop with her.

The drive to Portland was pleasantly uneventful, and Annie didn't want to spoil the atmosphere by bringing up Mary Beth's financial troubles. Instead, she asked about something she knew always made Mary Beth happy.

"How's Amy doing?"

As she expected, Mary Beth beamed at the mention of her niece.

"Great, as always. She's still spending a lot of time with Everett Graber, who works in the same office."

"Oh, and he has the cutest little boy."

"Peter. Yes, he's precious. I'd sure love to see them get a little closer one day. I guess Amy's still not ready for that."

"I know you miss having her around. Is she going to come visit this summer?"

Mary Beth pressed her lips together. "I hope she will. Every time Amy makes plans to come, Melanie figures out something for her to do instead. It's so frustrating."

Annie glanced briefly at her. "You know she's jealous of you, don't you? Melanie, I mean."

"Of me?" Mary Beth laughed. "You've seen her—tall and thin and still gorgeous. She is always fashionable, and always in the middle of some important national or international event. Not to mention being pretty well off. Why should she be jealous of me?"

"Because she knows Amy is closer to you than to her."

"Amy's her daughter, not mine."

"That's the point." Annie glanced up to make sure she hadn't missed her exit. "Amy is her daughter, but Amy loves you best."

Mary Beth smiled, but shook her head. "I don't know about that."

"I think I do. You're the one who's always been there for her. You're the one who wants her to be happy as she is without trying to make her into something she's not."

"Annie—"

"I'm not saying she doesn't love her mother. I'm sure she does. And I'm sure Melanie loves her. But you and Amy have a special relationship, and I think that's why Melanie gets jealous."

Mary Beth didn't say anything for a moment.

"I guess I've pretty much thought the same thing." She leaned her elbow on the armrest, propped her chin on her hand and looked out the window. "There wasn't much friction between us when we were growing up. I didn't even try to get into her spotlight, so we were OK. Mother groomed her for the high life, and I never really fit in there. That was OK, too, until Amy came along. She's just never been the society type either, so we always clicked. I haven't tried to take Melanie's place with her. It just sort of ... happened."

"You know, instead of resenting you, Melanie could always try to work on her relationship with Amy."

Mary Beth snorted. "That would involve cutting down on the cocktail parties and Broadway premieres and trips to Cannes."

"So what does she expect you to do? Pull away from Amy? And where would that leave Amy? She would be left without either of you."

"I know. But it's hard sometimes. I don't like conflict, especially in the family." She exhaled heavily. "Melanie called me the other day. I told Amy that I might have to sell out, and evidently she suggested that her mother could buy the building and rent it to me at what I'm paying now."

"That sounds reasonable. Can't she afford it?"

"I'm sure she could, but she told me in no uncertain

terms that she wouldn't even consider it. I told *her* in no uncertain terms that I wouldn't ever expect her to. And then she hung up on me."

"Oh dear."

Annie didn't know what else to say. Mary Beth asked so little of anyone. Would it have killed her sister to at least be nice to her?

"I just always thought I was an embarrassment to her, you know? Not stylish enough. Too middle class." There was a little catch in Mary Beth's voice. "I guess I've always known it was about Amy too."

"You know, it's not your fault if Melanie doesn't make time for her own child."

Mary Beth sniffed. "I suppose not."

She was quiet for a long time, and then she looked over at Annie.

"But if you want to know the ugly truth, I guess I've always liked knowing there's something special between Amy and me. I didn't plan on spending my life alone."

If she hadn't been driving, Annie would have reached over and hugged her. "You know you're not alone, Mary Beth. What would Stony Point be without you? I thought Peggy was going to start crying right there at the club meeting when you told us you might lose the shop. You don't think she was that upset just because she was afraid she wouldn't have someplace close to shop for quilting supplies, do you?"

Mary Beth only shrugged, but she smiled too.

"Whatever happens," Annie assured her, "we're behind you. Oh, and I just missed my exit."

This time Mary Beth laughed. "Don't worry. That antique shop isn't going anywhere."

"I know, but maybe our next clue will be there. I'm dying to find out."

"Just don't get too excited. Getting there a few minutes sooner or later isn't going to make any difference, and it's sure not worth a speeding ticket."

"I'm not speeding." Annie gave her a mischievous grin. "But my mind and heart are racing."

Mary Beth's eyes sparkled. "Mine too. I can't wait to find out if that key fits."

— 8 —

*P*ark Cambridge Antique Shoppe was one of a row of fashionable antique stores. Annie couldn't help smiling when she walked into it. Everything was set up as if the store was actually a home from the distant past. Antique kitchens were fully stocked. Antique bedrooms contained beds that were covered with delicate linens, perfectly preserved, and washstands with pitchers, and shaving brushes and mugs, and dressing tables with fine crocheted doilies and grand old perfume bottles and old costume jewelry. She could have spent hours exploring. Unfortunately, the visit lasted only as long as it took for them to talk to the manager, a girl who looked as if she was too young to be doing more than taking orders at the local Burly Boy's. But she was friendly and professional, and she seemed to know her business.

"Oh yes," she said with a flash of perfect teeth, "I do remember that desk. Beautiful old piece. I didn't think it would last long here, but I didn't even get it unloaded before someone bought it."

Mary Beth's shoulders sagged.

"Already?" Annie asked. "Is it possible to find out who?"

The girl looked at her warily. "We're really not supposed to say."

"We don't want you to get in trouble, but it's very

important. My friend here used to own the desk. Until a couple of weeks ago, in fact. It's been in her family at least since the 1860s. Anyway, she sold it to Kelsey's Odds and Ends, and he's the one who sold it to you. We think there might be some important family papers in the desk. All we want to do is check."

The girl looked at her sharply. Then her face softened, and she gave Annie one of the many business cards paper clipped to her order book. "I'm sure he just bought it to flip it anyway."

Mary Beth frowned. "Flip it?"

"Turn around and sell it again right away," the girl explained. "It happens a lot in our business, especially if he's planning to take it to New York, or if he already has a buyer for it."

There was worry in Mary Beth's eyes. "Oh Annie, you don't think he's already sold it again, do you?"

"Don't worry now." Annie gave her an encouraging smile. "Even if he did, we can trace it down again. Don't worry."

They thanked the girl and headed back to the car.

"Where now?" Mary Beth asked. "Is the next shop close?"

Annie squinted at the miniature map on the back of the business card. "Not really."

*   *   *   *

Annie glanced at the address on the business card one last time and then pushed open the door. Frank Sanders's

Antiques and Oddities was an overcrowded little storefront on a side street far from Park Cambridge's exclusive neighborhood. There seemed to be no rhyme or reason to how the merchandise was laid out, but it was fascinating all the same. A pair of men's boots that must have been over a hundred years old were sitting in a cut-glass punch bowl. One of them was topped with a rag doll with an embroidered face and yarn hair. Judging from the faded and yellowed fabrics, it could have been made about the same time as the boots. The other boot supported a ladies' coal-scuttle bonnet trimmed in silk ribbons that must have once been vivid crimson. It didn't look a day over a hundred and thirty.

The whole shop was a jumbled heap with what looked like costly pieces obscured by trinkets that had nothing to recommend them except their age.

Mary Beth looked around warily. "I don't see the desk."

"It could be anywhere in this mess." Annie went a little further into the shop. "Hello? Anybody here?"

She and Mary Beth waited a moment. Then Mary Beth came a little closer to Annie.

"He shouldn't leave all this unattended. Some of it looks really valuable."

"Hello?" Annie called again. "Mr. Sanders?"

"I suppose it's possible the owner or manager isn't actually Mr. Sanders. This place looks like it's been here a long time. Maybe the name's just been passed down." Mary Beth fingered a dish towel that had been embroidered with the word "MONDAY" and a picture of a washtub that looked like it might be from the 1930s. "I'd go crazy if my place was this disorganized. How does he even know what he has for sale? I can't imagine what he must be like himself."

Annie grinned a little. She couldn't help picturing Frank Sanders as a stooped, sixtyish little man in a snagged sweater of some indefinable color. He should have Coke-bottle glasses and Albert Einstein hair,—maybe with a cigarette hanging out of his mouth and wearing one of those old-time green eyeshades. She was thinking of stereotypical pawn shop managers, but still—

"May I help you?"

Annie and Mary Beth both turned at the low, cultured voice.

"We're looking for Frank Sanders," Mary Beth said.

The man smiled. "I'm Frank. What can I do for you?"

He was not very tall, likely in his mid-thirties, neatly groomed and wearing a sports coat with an open-neck shirt. He was too bland and geeky to be handsome, but he seemed pleasant enough.

Annie returned the smile. "We just came from Park Cambridge Antiques. The young lady there said you recently bought a cherry writing desk from her. We think it was made sometime around 1850. Does that sound familiar?"

The man nodded, his thick, sandy hair nodding with him. "Oh yeah. I remember that one very well, but it's not for sale. I've been looking for a piece like that for a long time now. The 1850s and '60s are a special interest of mine, and that one's going home with me. But I have plenty of other things I could show you."

"No, thank you. But would it be possible for us to just see the desk for a minute?"

Sanders still smiled, but he looked a little wary now. "See it?"

Mary Beth held out her hand. "My name is Mary Beth Brock. That desk has been in my family since before the Civil War."

He took the hand she offered and released it quickly. "I'm sorry, Ms. Brock, but my understanding is that you sold that desk outright. Janet at Park Cambridge sold it to me. I really couldn't think of selling it back."

"No, no, and I wouldn't ask that of you. I just think I might have left some family papers in it and was hoping you'd let us have a look."

"Papers?" His eyes narrowed. "I don't know. Janet didn't mention any papers."

"I don't even know if there are any papers," Mary Beth admitted. "But I'd like to check."

His smile brightened. "Oh well, of course."

"Don't forget the key," Annie prompted, and Mary Beth immediately started rummaging in her purse.

"We, um, found an old key we think goes to that desk, and we'd like to see if it fits."

"No problem." Sanders motioned for them to follow as he walked toward the back of the shop. "But it's not locked."

"Yes, I know. It was never locked as far as I know, not in my lifetime anyway, and I think I took everything out of it before I sold it. Since I have the key now, at least what I think might be the key, I just want to make sure I haven't missed anything."

"Sounds fair enough."

Sanders led them through an office that was even more

cluttered than the shop and back into a warehouse area. It was amazingly neat and well ordered. Annie gave Mary Beth a "Who knew?" glance, but she managed to hold her tongue. The desk was near the loading dock.

"There she is. I was about to put it into my truck." Sanders looked sympathetic. "I have to tell you, though, I went over it pretty thoroughly after I bought it. Some of these pieces have the most interesting little drawers and cubbies. Everything in this one was empty."

Annie and Mary Beth both started examining the desk, opening drawers and cabinet doors. As he said, and as they had suspected, it was empty. The only keyhole was to a lock on a cabinet door on the right side of the desk. It was maybe five inches square.

"At least try the key," Annie suggested.

Mary Beth fumbled with the little brass key, but it fit into the hole with a minimal amount of wiggling. In another moment there was a gratifying click, and the door was locked. With another click, it opened again. It was still empty.

Mary Beth sighed.

Sanders pointed to the open cabinet. "I suppose you checked in the back in there."

"In the back?" Mary Beth and Annie said at the same time.

"Sure." Sanders reached in and, with a little jiggling, worked free a well-fitted false back inside the cabinet, revealing another cubbyhole behind it. "I've seen a number of these old beauties with hidden spaces."

"A deeper secret place," Mary Beth whispered.

Sanders's smile turned a little puzzled. "What?"

"Nothing, really." Annie felt inside. "It certainly is empty."

Mary Beth looked at Annie. "I don't know whether to be happy or sad. It's nice to know this is the right key, I guess. But the next clue—"

"Probably gone a long time ago." Annie patted her arm. "Oh well, it was fun anyway."

"I'm sorry you didn't find what you were looking for. If there's anything else I can do, let me know."

Mary Beth nodded.

"And if you have any other great pieces from this period, I'd love to take a look at them. As you can see, I like a big variety."

Annie laughed. "I don't know how you keep track of everything you have. Or how your customers find anything."

"It's my own personal business theory. Let the customers uncover things for themselves. A shopping adventure. A treasure hunt, if you will." Sanders grinned, and for a minute he almost looked charming. "Everybody loves a treasure hunt."

Annie glanced at Mary Beth, and they both giggled.

"I suppose they do." Mary Beth glanced at the little brass key she still held, and then she handed it to Sanders. "I guess you'd better have this too. I don't need it anymore."

"Thanks." He slipped it into his pocket. "Now, Ms. Brock, tell me about those other pieces you have from this same period."

"Not much of anything, I'm afraid. Some china, a mantel clock, an end table. I think the desk was really the nicest one, though the others are pretty enough."

He took a business card from his inside jacket pocket.

"Next time you decide to sell something, you call me first."

"Well ..."

"Promise?" Again he gave Mary Beth his almost-charming smile. "I guarantee you the best prices."

Mary Beth took the card, relenting. "*If* I decide to sell, I promise I'll give you a call."

"See you soon!" he called as they left the shop.

*   *   *   *

Mary Beth was surprised to find that "soon" for Frank Sanders meant at six thirty the next evening.

"Mr. Sanders. I really didn't expect—"

He squinted a little in the late-day sun as he stood there on her front porch. "I hope you'll forgive me, Ms. Brock, but I was out this way, and I thought I'd take a chance and see if you might be in."

She knew she hadn't given her address or anything. How in the world—?

"How did you find me?"

Sanders looked a little sheepish. "I just looked up your name on the Internet. You were the only one in the area where Bob Kelsey would be doing business. I figured it had to be you."

"I see."

"So ... may I come in? I'd love to see those other pieces you were telling me about yesterday."

"Well, I really have plans." *Plans to not let an unexpected stranger into the house.* "If I decide to sell any of my things, I'll make sure to let you know first."

"Just for a minute." He gave her an ingratiating smile. "I wasn't going to stop, and I know I should have called ahead. I don't get out this way often, and I just couldn't help myself. I promise not to keep you."

"Well... ."

"Just for a minute," he wheedled. "I love the period just before the Civil War, and your desk is such a great example of it. I just want a peek at the other things you have."

Mary Beth looked at him for a long minute, and then she exhaled. "Let me just make a quick phone call."

"Great. Thanks."

She hurried inside and speed-dialed Annie's number.

"Hi. It's Mary Beth. I thought you'd be here by now."

Of course, Annie sounded puzzled. "You did?"

"Yeah, you're on your way, aren't you?"

"What's going on?"

Mary Beth smiled and nodded at her unexpected visitor though the screen door. "No, of course we're not going to cancel, Annie. Mr. Sanders from the shop in Portland just dropped by to see what else I had from my great-great-grandmother. I just figured you were running a little late and wanted you to know there was no hurry."

"You mean you want me to come over as soon as I can, right?" There was concern in Annie's voice. "Are you OK?"

"Oh sure. I'll see you in a few minutes then."

— 9 —

*M*ary Beth hung up the phone and opened the door for Frank Sanders.

"I don't want to spoil your plans." He smiled, already focused on the end table with the lions on it. "This is great. Judging by the age of it, I'd say you must have gotten this from your great-great-grandmother as well. What would you take for it?"

"I don't think I want to sell it right now," Mary Beth told him. "As I said before, I'll let you know when I'm ready. *If* I'm ever ready."

He laughed. "You have to excuse me, Ms. Brock. Sometimes I find a piece that just speaks to me. May I move these things off of it?"

Mary Beth cleared the table for him, and he spent some time examining it. She didn't feel he needed to know about the opening in the pedestal. By the time he was looking at her mantel clock, Annie was at the door.

"Annie! Come in." Mary Beth half dragged her into the living room. "You remember Mr. Sanders from yesterday, don't you?"

Annie offered him her hand. "Of course. What a surprise, Mr. Sanders."

He chuckled. "That's what Ms. Brock said. But I hope she's forgiven me for dropping in on her. You know, this clock is fabulous." He fished a little digital camera out of his coat pocket. "And I'd like to get a couple of pictures, if you don't mind."

Of all the things passed down to her, Mary Beth had always been proudest of the clock in particular. It was made of cherry wood like the desk and was rectangular in shape, only about fifteen inches high and ten inches wide. The clock face was round, centered in the top half of the clock as if it were the sun shining down on a forest glade. It even had little rays coming out from it, widening as they came closer to the ground. The pendulum was in the shape of a small dove that looked as if it were flying over the carved grass and flowers, and peeping out of the foliage were a tiny rabbit and two squirrels. At the bottom, a doe lay watching as her twin fawns slept against her. On either side of the clock and going around to the back, were sturdy carved oaks, and here and there, birds nesting in the leafy branches. Below everything was a base of solid wood, about three inches high, delicately inlaid with teak and mother-of-pearl. It was a work of art.

Sanders examined it and took pictures from all sides, and with Mary Beth's reluctant permission, he even took the back off to look at the works.

"It's obviously from the mid-1800s like the other things. Gorgeous carvings, and it's still in amazing condition too."

He quoted her a nice price.

Mary Beth glanced at Annie. "No, I don't think so. I want to hang on to this, even if I have to sell some other things."

Sanders nodded. "It's a one of a kind, for certain. I know

about a few woodcarvers from this period, but it doesn't look like the work of anyone I've seen. It keeps good time?"

"Excellent. I set all my other clocks by it."

He increased his offer by half, but Mary Beth shook her head. "I'm sorry. No. This clock has been in my family for over a hundred years. I can't let it go."

He gave her a hard glance and then doubled his most recent offer.

Mary Beth bit her lip. It was tempting. So tempting.

"No," she said finally. "I just can't. I appreciate it, but no."

"Too bad."

Sanders looked disappointed, but he seemed in no hurry to leave. He still studied the clock, jotting down notes to himself about the carvings and the works.

"I'm going to see if I can find out more about whoever made this."

"If you do, I'd love to know about it," Mary Beth told him. "I've always wondered."

He was bold enough to help himself to the rest of the living and dining room, commenting on various items he found there, offering to buy a few pieces, but eventually Mary Beth herded him toward the door. "I appreciate your generosity, but, really, I don't want to sell anything right now."

"Too bad," Sanders said again, "but you know how to reach me if you do."

With a nod at Annie, he finally left.

Mary Beth locked her door behind him and then sank down on the couch. "Sorry to put you in a spot like that, Annie, but thanks for coming."

"He just showed up and wanted to come in?"

"Yeah. I mean, I'm sure he's harmless enough, but I didn't really want to let him in knowing I was here by myself."

Annie sat down beside her. "I'm glad I could help you out. He sure did like your clock, but who could blame him?"

Mary Beth grinned. "It is a beautiful old thing, isn't it?"

"He offered a pretty good price for it too."

"I know." Mary Beth frowned. "I just couldn't sell it. Even his last offer would be only enough to postpone the inevitable. And if I have to lose the shop, I don't want to lose the last of my heirlooms as well."

Annie hesitated for a moment. "How are things going with the shop?"

Mary Beth shook her head, afraid for a moment she might cry, but she managed a smile instead. "Nothing's changed. Either I find a miracle by the end of next month or Stony Point gets a Burly Boy's Burger Barn."

"Is there anything I can do?"

She knew Annie meant it, that she'd help however she could, if she possibly could. Too bad it wasn't that simple.

"Just keep praying for that miracle."

"I've been doing that all along." There was a twinkle in Annie's emerald eyes. "All of us have."

"For now, how about having a cup of coffee with me? It's the least I can do after dragging you over here without a moment's notice."

"Thanks, but I really don't have time to—" Annie frowned at the clock on the mantel. "I think it's stopped."

Mary Beth growled half under her breath. "That little pip-squeak. What did he do? That clock never stops."

She went to the mantel, gave the clock's pendulum a gentle push and was rewarded with a satisfying ticking sound.

"I'm sure he didn't mean to mess it up," Annie soothed. "You saw how interested he was in it. 'Fascinated' might be a better word."

Mary Beth came back to the sofa and sat down. "I'm sure you're right. I could tell he was trying to be careful when he looked at it, even if he did practically take the thing apart. But, still, he shouldn't—"

The clock wasn't ticking any more.

Mary Beth bit her lip, figuratively biting her tongue at the same time. "OK, one more try."

She started the clock again. It managed a few strong ticks and then fell silent.

"Why don't we take it down from the mantel and look it over?" Annie suggested. "If the mechanism is over a 150 years old, it can't be very complicated."

They did just that, but neither of them could find anything wrong.

"It doesn't look as if anything is broken." Mary Beth moved the light a little closer to the back of the clock. It was the one she used for fine needlework, and it was bright and clear—perfect for the task. "It does look a little dusty in there."

"Maybe a good cleaning and a tune-up is all it needs."

Mary Beth shook her head. "I'm sure you're right. I guess it's going to have to sit still for a while until I can get it looked at by a real clockmaker."

"I tell you what," Annie said. "I'm supposed to go into Brunswick on Friday. How about letting me take it with me to the clock shop there? They'll probably want to keep it for a week or two, but I know they'll do a good job. I've taken some of Gram's things there for repairs in the past. Mr. Malcolm is a genius with antiques."

"You know I can't do it right now, Annie."

"I know you have the shop open during the day. That's why I'll be happy to take it for you."

"I appreciate it, but it's not the lack of time that's the problem. I wish it was only that."

"Oh." Annie looked a little flustered. "Listen, I know what this clock means to you. Why don't you let me take it in? My treat."

"Do you know what repairs on these things cost?"

"I have a pretty good idea. I had to get some of Gram's things fixed too. Come on, Mary Beth. Let me do one nice thing for you."

"This isn't the same thing as springing for lunch, you know. It might cost three or four hundred dollars to fix it." Mary Beth frowned, thinking of Frank Sanders. "Besides, you're not the one who broke it."

"I don't think it's really broken. Just out of whack some-where. And like you said, it does need cleaning. When was the last time somebody looked at it?"

"Never," Mary Beth admitted. "Not since I've had it anyway. I know it could use some fixing up, but I can't let you pay for it. It's too expensive."

She felt herself weakening though. She did love the clock, and it would be so nice to have something good happen right now.

"An heirloom like that ought to be taken good care

of." Annie put her arm through Mary Beth's and squeezed tightly. "Come on, let me take it. If you have to, you can pay me back when you're rich and famous."

Mary Beth swallowed hard. Then, with a laugh, she pushed free and stood up, blinking hard. "Annie Dawson, you are *not* going to do this to me. You're not going to make me cry over that dumb clock."

"You know this isn't about the clock, which certainly isn't dumb, by the way." Annie looked at her almost reprovingly. "You don't realize how much we all love you, and you ought to. You're worth every bit of it."

Mary Beth looked down at the table, knowing her face was flushed, but unable to decide if it was from embarrassment or pleasure. Maybe it was a little of both.

"Now," Annie said softly. "You're going to let me take your clock with me on Friday, right?"

"No, really, Annie. You're so sweet to offer, but I can't let you spend that much. It's crazy."

Annie thought for a minute. "What if I just take it for an estimate? I'm going to be right there anyway. The worst that could happen is that I'll bring it back to you like it is. No harm, no foul, right?"

Mary Beth nodded her head, laughing. "Just an estimate. I mean it."

Annie grinned.

* * * *

As planned, Annie took the clock to Brunswick on Friday. Mr. Malcolm at the repair shop was almost as fascinated with the clock as Frank Sanders had been. The estimate he gave her for repairs and cleaning was fairly broad and contingent on what he found when he made a detailed examination, but he told her he would call when they had more specific information, and if she decided to proceed, she would probably be able to pick up the clock in two weeks.

When she got back home to Grey Gables, Alice rushed out of the carriage house next door to meet her.

"You'll never believe what happened. Mary Beth's house was broken into."

"No!" Annie scrambled out of her car. "As if she didn't have enough to worry about. Poor thing. Is she all right?"

"Hanging in there. She was at the shop, of course, so she didn't know until she got home. Her window was broken out, the one by the back door in her dining room. Whoever it was just let himself in."

"Did he clean out everything?"

"It's funny. Mary Beth says there wasn't anything taken that was worth much—a pack of soft drinks from the fridge, a box of cookies and a couple of bags of chips and her CD player and DVD/VCR. I don't remember what else. Not much."

Annie scowled. "Kids, I bet. Poor Mary Beth—everything seems to be happening to her right now. Do you think she could use some company?"

"We can always call up and ask. Maybe we could take over a few things and make a little dinner party for her. It might cheer her up."

Annie smiled. "It won't hurt to ask. Come inside, and let's see what she says."

Annie called right away; Mary Beth sounded exhausted and a little overwhelmed, but she seemed glad for the company and the knowledge that she wouldn't have to worry about fixing anything for herself for dinner.

"Well," Annie said once she had hung up the phone, "that's settled. Now what can we make to cheer up Mary Beth?"

*　*　*　*

Mary Beth was just finishing tidying up her ransacked kitchen and living room when her doorbell rang. She glanced at her dining room table, checking to see that the three place settings had the appropriate number of knives and forks and spoons, and that a crisp spring-pink napkin was folded beside each plate. The only real tangible reminder of the break-in was the gap on her living room shelf where her CD and DVD players had once sat and the broken dining room window. Wally had made her laugh when he came to board it up, asking her if he should set up a regular glass-replacement appointment for her from here forward.

She was trying to be thankful that the break-in was no worse, but piled on top of everything else, it was hard to do. Annie and Alice would cheer her up, though. And both of them were terrific cooks.

"Coming!"

She flung open the door and stopped short.

"Mr. Sanders."

"Yeah, I know. Twice in the same week is a little bit much." He shrugged and smiled. "I don't mean to be a pest, but I was in Stony Point again, and I thought I'd take another look at your clock. I think I have the maker narrowed down to one of three from that era in Virginia, but there are a few details I wanted to make sure I got right. And I'd like to check for some particular maker's marks too."

Mary Beth pressed her lips together and dredged up a regretful smile. "I'm sorry, but the clock isn't here right now. And this really isn't a good time. I'm expecting company."

He followed her glance through the living room to the dining room table. His eyes widened when he noticed the boarded up window.

"Oh man. What happened to your window?" He looked around the living room a little more. "A break-in?"

"I'm afraid so."

"Then the clock was stolen?"

"No, I'm thankful to say, my friend Annie took it to Brunswick for repairs."

He looked relieved. "Well, that's good news. It would be a shame to lose something like that. You didn't have any of your other antiques stolen, did you?"

"No," she assured him, amused in spite of herself by his single-mindedness. "And I will absolutely call you first if I decide to sell any of them."

They both turned when Alice's red Mustang pulled into the driveway.

"There's my company." She waved toward the car. "Now, if you'll excuse me."

"Sure." He padded down the porch steps. "But you'll let me know, right?"

"You'll be the very first."

He gave Annie a little wave as he passed her, and then he was gone.

"Him again?" Annie giggled. "I think he has a crush on you."

"Very funny." Mary Beth tried to lift up the corner of the aluminum foil that covered the casserole dish Annie carried. "And this is … ?"

"No peeking," Alice scolded, getting between her and Annie, "or you don't get any of this."

She held up a covered pie dish, and Mary Beth hurried back up to open the front door for them.

"So what did your stalker want?" Alice set down her pie dish and a plastic bag full of other goodies. "He's persistent, isn't he?"

"Last thing I needed today." Mary Beth rolled her eyes when the telephone rang. "Excuse me—I'll be right back."

"We'll just get everything on the table," Alice said. "Take your time."

Dinner was ready to serve by the time Mary Beth came back, but by then she wasn't very interested in eating.

"That was Chief Edwards. He said they found my DVD and CD players all smashed up and thrown in one of those dumpsters out behind the Grand Avenue Fish House. At least he's pretty sure they're mine. They're the same models, and it would be an awfully big coincidence for two just like mine to show up just now. Based on the other trash in the dumpster, he's sure they were put in there today. Why would anyone steal something like that just so they could smash it all up and throw it away?"

Alice shrugged. "Cold feet? If it was kids who broke in

here, maybe they decided they didn't want to get caught with stolen goods. Did Chief Edwards say they found any fingerprints?"

Mary Beth's mouth turned down. "Wiped clean. Evidently, not even mine are on there anymore."

"That's just a shame." Annie shook her head. "You know, it just doesn't make sense. Why *did* they break in?"

～ 10 ～

Annie stepped inside the clock shop, charmed as always by all the little ticks and whirrs and bells that greeted her. It was almost like stepping into a meadow full of birds, cheery and busy. When Mr. Malcolm called her the week before to give her the estimate for the repair, she had immediately told him to go ahead. The cost wasn't quite as high as she had expected, and she was more determined than ever to have something positive happen to Mary Beth. This would cheer her up some, and that would make it worth every penny it cost. Mary Beth would be so surprised when she brought the clock back, working again and running like new.

Mr. Malcolm looked up from his desk where he was examining a little brass-and-ivory clock no more than four inches high, and his rheumy eyes brightened.

"Ah, Mrs. Dawson." He put down the jeweler's glass he was using. "Good to see you. How can I help you?"

"I came to pick up Mary Beth's clock. The one with the forest scene carved into it."

"Oh, that one. That's a real beauty. But, I'm sorry you came all the way here. Mrs. Brock's husband picked it up this morning."

"Her *husband*!?"

"Yes. I wasn't here, but my assistant said he was a very

nice fellow. He said he wanted to surprise her. I'm sorry
he didn't let you in on it though. It would have saved you
a trip."

Annie could only stare at him, open mouthed. "Her
husband?"

"Yes. Is something wrong?"

"Mary Beth doesn't have a husband, Mr. Malcolm."

Mr. Malcolm didn't say anything for a moment. "And I
suppose you still have the claim slip?"

Annie dug it out of her purse.

"I'm so sorry, Mrs. Dawson. I wasn't here this morning.
My staff has strict instructions not to release any repair
items without a slip." He got up and retrieved a ledger book
from the counter behind him and opened it to the last used
page. Then he picked up the telephone on his desk and
pressed the third button at the bottom. "Jennifer, may I see
you a moment?"

The girl who came from the back of the shop was young,
probably not long out of school, and she couldn't stop apol-
ogizing. She was almost in tears.

"I didn't know. He described the clock to me and said it
belonged to Mrs. Brock. Then when I told him that wasn't
the name it was under, he said he remembered that you
had brought it, Mrs. Dawson, and he gave me your name.
I thought it was OK. He paid for the repair. I didn't think
he'd do that unless it was his." She bit her high-gloss lip. "I
didn't know."

"What did he look like, Jennifer?" Mr. Malcolm was being extremely patient. Annie was glad he was being kind to
the girl, but she hoped he realized this was an extremely

serious matter too. Mary Beth would be heartbroken.

Jennifer only shrugged her slim shoulders. "I don't know. Just a guy."

"Was he young or old?" Annie asked.

"Sorta old." The girl thought for a moment more. "Yeah, he was sorta old. Probably as old as my dad—forty or fifty or something."

Annie managed to not roll her eyes. "What color was his hair?"

"Umm ... kinda brownish blond, I guess."

Annie had a terrible thought. Frank Sanders might be as old as forty, and he had sandy blond hair.

"What there was of it," Jennifer continued.

Annie shook her head. "What do you mean? He was bald?"

"Yeah, pretty much He had one of those little fringe thingies around his head and then like three strands across the top. Do guys really think that helps?"

Hmmm. The hair didn't sound much like Sanders's, but the rest of the girl's description wasn't very precise either. He wanted the clock. It had been obvious from everything he had said, from the way he looked at it. Could he have been so brazen as to just take it?

"What else do you remember about him?" Annie asked.

"Kinda tall, I think."

Annie frowned. She would never categorize Sanders as tall. Maybe the girl's estimation of "kinda tall" was about as accurate as her idea of "sorta old."

"Do you remember the color of his eyes?" Mr. Malcolm asked. "Or anything else specific about him?"

"I'm really sorry. I just don't. He came in and paid for the clock and left."

"I don't suppose he paid with a check or credit card," Annie asked, hoping Sanders would turn out to be the stupidest criminal in the world, but she wasn't surprised to see the girl shake her head.

"Just cash. Tens and twenties."

Mr. Malcolm smiled at Annie apologetically. "All right, Jennifer. We'll talk about this in a few minutes."

"I'm so sorry," the girl said again, looking as if she might cry, and then she scurried into the back of the shop.

"The daughter of one of my niece's friends," he said. "Two years of junior college and no experience. I thought I could help."

Annie felt bad for both of them. "She'll learn. In the meantime, I suppose we'd better call the police." She stopped for a minute, thinking. "No, maybe we can get this cleared up without involving them. If the man who picked up the clock is who I think he is, then I know right where to find him. Do you think I could talk to Jennifer again?"

Mr. Malcolm looked puzzled, but he smiled. "Of course."

*   *   *   *

Jennifer was more than willing to help. Her cooperation was mostly to atone for allowing the clock to be stolen, Annie was sure. But she was glad to have Jennifer along.

Annie glanced over at her as she started the car. "All you have to do when we get there is look around the shop as if you're looking for something to buy. Then, if you see the man who picked up the clock, let me know."

The girl nodded, and then her big blue eyes pooled with tears. "Mrs. Dawson, I feel so bad about what happened. I would never have let him have it if he hadn't known your name and all about the clock."

"We'll get it worked out, Jennifer. Don't you worry. And you know what? Now you have some valuable business experience." Annie smiled at her and gave her a comforting pat. "And we're going to get that clock back. You just watch."

*   *   *   *

As soon as she and Jennifer went into Frank Sanders's shop, Annie started searching the jumbled shelves for any sign of Mary Beth's clock. Surely he wouldn't have it there in plain sight. It was most likely at his home by now, part of his private collection of pieces that "spoke to him." Still, she kept looking.

Jennifer wandered toward the middle of the shop to look at an ornate English wardrobe carved with birds and animals and trees, a rising sun and intertwined rings and crowns.

"Lovely piece, isn't it?"

Annie glanced over at the sound of Frank Sanders's voice.

Jennifer was smiling at him, nothing in her expression to show that she recognized him or that he recognized her.

"Oh yes, it is. I ... I'm really just looking though. My mom's birthday is in a couple of weeks, and I'd like to find something nice for her."

Sanders smiled too. "I'm sure we can find something

she would like. Does she— Well, hello, Mrs. Dawson. What a surprise to see you here again!" He turned back to Jennifer. "She's not your mother, is she?"

"Oh no. Actually, I work at—"

"We're just friends, Mr. Sanders," Annie said. "Although I do have some kind of sad news."

"What's that?"

"You remember my friend, Mary Beth Brock? You were very interested in her mantel clock, the one with all the beautiful carving."

"Oh, certainly. I won't soon forget that piece. Really exquisite."

Annie nodded, watching his eyes. "I'm afraid it was stolen."

He looked dismayed. "Stolen? I know her home was broken into, but she said the clock—"

"Was being repaired, yes. It seems that someone stole it from the repair shop."

"Oh dear. That's a shame. I hope it was insured. Or at least that the repair shop will pay her the value of it. Too bad she didn't take my offer while she could. It was twice what insurance will give her. Maybe three times."

"It was the strangest thing," Annie said. "Whoever came and got the clock was pretending he was Mary Beth's husband. And when he found the repair wasn't in her name, he gave mine instead. Isn't it odd that someone like that would know both our names—and know that the clock was being repaired?"

Sanders stared at her for a moment and then laughed gruffly. "Are you saying you think I'm mixed up in this?"

"I couldn't help but notice how badly you wanted that clock. I don't know who else would have known it was in the shop and known my name and Mary Beth's."

"That's hardly proof, you know. When did I supposedly perpetrate this crime?"

"This morning. About ten thirty."

He went behind the counter, brought out a metal waste-paper basket and dug through it briefly. Then he handed her a boarding pass. "As you can see, I was in New York City from this past Monday until takeoff at 10:48 this morning. It took me some time to deplane and get my luggage and get the shuttle back to where I had parked my car. I only got back to the shop a little while ago."

Annie studied the boarding pass. It certainly seemed legitimate. If the clock had been taken at 10:30, there was no way he could have been on that flight in New York at 10:48.

She glanced at Jennifer who gave her a subtle shake of the head. Obviously, Sanders wasn't the man she had seen at the repair shop.

Annie thrust the boarding pass back into his hand. "That doesn't mean you didn't have someone take it for you."

Again he laughed ruefully. "I suppose that's a possibility, but is it really all that practical? I'll admit I was smitten with that clock. It was absolutely unique, and I've been in this business a long time now. But even at the inflated price I offered your friend, it's not worth me going to jail for, now is it?"

Annie looked at him, trying hard not to glare. He had a point. But there were just too many coincidences at work here for her to believe he wasn't involved.

He finally smiled at her. "I can understand your suspicions. Really, I can. But, as you see, I just couldn't have done it. And I would have been very stupid if I had."

"I guess that's one point we can agree on." Annie tugged Jennifer's arm. "We'd better go."

"I'd still be happy to help you find something for your mother, young lady," Sanders offered.

Jennifer only shrugged. "I haven't really decided what I want to get yet. Maybe I'll come back sometime."

"You're always welcome. And Mrs. Dawson, no hard feelings, eh?"

Annie merely glanced at the hand he offered. "I'm not sure about that yet."

She hurried Jennifer out to the car and sped out of the parking lot.

"You're sure he wasn't at the repair shop this morning?"

"No. He's definitely not the man I saw."

"Have you ever seen him?"

"No. I mean, I guess I could have passed him on the street or something, but I don't remember ever seeing him."

Annie drove for a few minutes in silence, heading back to Mr. Malcolm's repair shop to drop Jennifer off. Then she made an abrupt U-turn.

"Where are we going?" the girl asked.

"There's been a theft. We are sure of that much. If you don't mind, we're going to go report it to the police."

~ 11 ~

It was getting late when Annie finally returned to Stony Point. She had told Mary Beth she was picking up the clock, and Mary Beth had told her to just come drop it off on her way back. Now, Annie hated showing up empty-handed.

No, it wasn't just that. It was that Mary Beth had already had enough happening to her right now. She didn't need something else piled on top of it.

Once she had brought Jennifer back to Mr. Malcolm's shop from the police station, Annie had considered calling Mary Beth from the clock shop to break the bad news to her, but somehow that felt cowardly. Besides, taking the clock to Mr. Malcolm had been Annie's idea. Instead, she called up to ask if she could drop by Mary Beth's house. It was only right that she should have to tell Mary Beth about the loss of the clock herself in person.

"It's open," Mary Beth called when Annie knocked. "Come on in."

Annie did.

"You know, you're pretty trusting for someone who just got burgled."

Mary Beth laughed. "I just unlocked it a minute ago. I figured you'd be here about now. What's the big news you couldn't tell me over the phone?"

"Can we sit down for a minute?"

"Sure." Mary Beth gestured to the sofa. "I know you like mysteries, but I'll take my news straight up, if you don't mind."

"OK." Annie steeled herself and then plowed ahead. "You know I took your clock to get an estimate for the repairs, and they called me to let me know how much it would be."

Mary Beth lifted one eyebrow. "Yes? Was it that bad?"

"No, actually. It wasn't as much as I had expected, and I told them to go ahead and fix it. I wanted to surprise you."

Mary Beth's face lit. "Really? Oh Annie, you shouldn't have done it. It's much too generous of you."

"I went to pick it up earlier today."

Mary Beth looked at Annie expectantly. "So? Where is it?"

"I'm so sorry, Mary Beth. I don't have it. Somebody stole it from the repair shop."

Mary Beth rolled her eyes. "Cute. Do you need me to help you get it out of the—" Her forehead wrinkled. "You're serious, aren't you?"

"I am *so* sorry. Mr. Malcolm wanted to call you to apologize, but I told him I should talk to you first."

"Was his place broken into also?"

"No." Annie took Mary Beth by the arm and sat down with her on the couch. "It's just really stupid. Some friend of his niece's just started working for him, and she let someone pick it up without the claim ticket. Someone who knew your name and mine."

Mary Beth frowned hard. "Frank Sanders."

"It almost has to be. I couldn't get much of a description from the girl, but I thought it could be Frank. She said he was about forty and tall."

"Tall?"

"OK, maybe she meant tallish. But she also said he was nearly bald. He's definitely not bald."

"Wouldn't be the first time a thieving little weasel wore a rug, you know."

Annie couldn't help laughing. "I'm glad you're not too mad about it."

"Oh, I'm plenty mad." Her voice shook a little in spite of her smile. "He struck me wrong from the minute we went into his shop, and now I know why. I think I'll just go pay Mr. Sanders a visit."

"That won't do any good. I already tried. The girl from the repair place and I went to his shop. She didn't recognize him."

"You're joking. Really?"

"Really. She's sure he wasn't the man who picked up the clock. And he showed me a boarding pass for a flight from New York City. It was for this morning. Sanders couldn't have been the one who got the clock."

Mary Beth scowled. "Then he had help."

"That's what I think too. But, really, as beautiful as it is, it's not *that* valuable. The police told me he doesn't have a criminal record apart from a couple of old safety-code violations for his shop, and he took care of those a long time ago. It's not like he routinely steals things and then sells them."

"No, but he wanted my clock. I could tell."

"That's obvious. But now we have to let the police take care of it."

Mary Beth nodded, calming. "I know you're right. I just can't believe the *nerve* of the man." She finally grinned. "I might just snatch that rug right off his head."

"Jennifer—that's the girl from the repair shop—and I already made a report." Annie dug in her purse and pulled out a business card. "This is the name of the officer we talked to. You'll have to give him a call. I'm sure you'll have to go file a complaint since it's your clock."

"All right."

"The officer is supposed to go talk to Mr. Sanders too. I don't know when that will be. I guess when he has time."

"OK."

"And I hope you don't mind, but I told him your house was broken into too."

Mary Beth started to nod, and then she looked at Annie. "You don't think that could have been Sanders, too, do you?"

"I don't know. It's possible."

"But he came back to look at the clock after the break in. He looked pretty surprised to find out it wasn't here."

"I know. Maybe that was all just to make him look innocent."

"I guess some thieving little weasels are good actors too." Mary Beth closed her eyes and took a deep breath. "At least it's a fairly simple fix. He ought to be in jail before the week's out."

"I don't think it's going to be that simple. There's just no evidence."

Mary Beth shook her head. "The police have ways of finding things out. He has to be involved somehow. Just wait and see."

*   *   *   *

"Nothing at all?" Annie wasn't surprised, but she was disappointed. "I was afraid of that."

"As he told you, he was in New York City that day. Most of the week, really." Mary Beth sighed and straightened one of the cozy armchairs in the middle of A Stitch in Time in preparation for that morning's meeting of the Hook and Needle Club. "Plus, he voluntarily let the police search his shop and his house, and they found nothing."

"That's no surprise."

"And the police even did what I suggested and made sure his hair was real."

Annie giggled.

"And Jennifer from Mr. Malcolm's shop told them, too, that she didn't recognize Sanders at all when the two of you were at his shop. They just don't have enough evidence to make an arrest." Mary Beth's eyes filled, and she blinked hard. "Neither do we."

"But we *know*." Annie doubled her fists, aching to pound something. "He *has* to be the one! It's just too much of a coincidence to imagine someone else is behind all this."

"But why would he take it?" Mary Beth asked. "I mean, it *is* obvious that he was interested in it. He told us how much he loves pieces from around the time of the Civil War. Why would he risk stealing the clock when he'd have to know we'd suspect him first?"

"That's not actual proof though. Not enough to go to court over."

"How could he have made sure I took the clock for repairs anyway? Maybe this isn't as obvious as we thought."

Annie scowled. "Easiest thing in the world. He comes

and looks at the clock and does something, I don't know what, to make it quit working. He's an antiques specialist. He's got to know a lot of things people do to make pieces seem more or less valuable than they actually are."

"I didn't see anything wrong with the clock," Mary Beth said. "Of course, what I know about clock mechanisms could be hidden in a thimble, but I looked it over pretty well when it stopped."

"And you didn't notice anything unusual?"

Mary Beth shook her head. "It looked all right to me. I guess he could have done something to affect it. But, if he did plan for it to have to go to the repair shop, how could he have known when it would be there? He knows I've been selling heirlooms to keep in business, so he knows I'm short of cash right now. How would he know I'd take it for an expensive repair right away like that? And to which shop?"

Annie sighed and settled into her favorite chair. "And if he fixed the clock so it wouldn't run, why would he break into the house after it was already gone?"

"Hmmm." Mary Beth shrugged. "Maybe the break-in really *was* kids, and maybe it didn't have anything to do with the clock."

"That's a pretty big coincidence, isn't it?"

"They do happen. Sometimes."

"I guess we'll have to pretend he didn't have anything to do with the break-in—for now. But if Frank Sanders was in New York all that day, and the girl from Mr. Malcolm's is sure he's not the one who picked up the clock, who was it? And why?"

"He had to know me and you, whoever he was. He mentioned us by name."

The bell over the front door jingled, and Alice swept into the shop carrying the bag that held her cross-stitch project and a larger bag with "Princessa" written in fuchsia across the side. "Oh good. I'm glad nobody's here yet."

Annie lifted one eyebrow, pretending to be offended. "Well, I like that."

"I mean nobody but us." There was a sparkle of mischief in Alice's blue eyes. "I had the greatest idea for you, Mary Beth."

"It doesn't involve selling jewelry or home decor, does it?"

"Only part of the time."

"Alice MacFarlane, I told you that kind of thing isn't for me. Now, please, just take all that back to your car."

"Just take a look. I promise you, this line will sell itself here. Look."

She opened one slender white box. Nestled on a strip of cotton padding was a silver charm bracelet.

"Oh, cute." Annie lifted the bracelet out of its box. "Look at that tiny little pair of scissors."

"And they open and close." Alice demonstrated. "But I think I like the spool the best."

Mary Beth took the bracelet, examining it, touching one finger to the little silver skein of embroidery floss and then to the tiny button next to it. "It is awfully cute. Some of the ones I've seen are just too big and junky looking. This one is beautifully made and really quite delicate."

"Does that mean you'll carry them in the shop?" Alice

lifted her eyebrows hopefully. "They're really popular right now."

"This is a needlework shop, not a jewelry store."

Mary Beth's tone was firm, but Alice was the consummate saleswoman.

"But you know women who do needlework will just eat this up. Come on. You want one yourself, don't you? I can tell you do. I know it's not much, but I thought it might in some tiny way help you keep the shop going until everything is settled one way or the other."

A touch of a smile tugged at the corner of Mary Beth's mouth. "They're awfully cute."

"And you'd get half the retail price in commissions. What do you say?"

"I don't know." Mary Beth glanced at Annie.

"What would it hurt to try?" Annie toyed with the bracelet Mary Beth still held, running her finger lightly under the dangling charms, making them dance. "I'll be your first customer."

Mary Beth closed her hand, and the dancing stopped. "No, really, I can't. I don't have time for this kind of thing. I don't want to be a Princessa rep or a rep for anybody. I don't want to sign up for anything or take training or go to meetings or—"

"No, no." Alice waived one hand to stop her. "You don't have to do any of that. I'll be the rep. I'll take care of the paperwork and ordering the merchandise and everything else. All you have to do is let these sit on your counter here— right where all the good little impulse items go—and sell themselves. You take half the money, and I send the rest to the company. Now what could be easier than that?"

Again Mary Beth glanced at Annie.

"Sounds like a great deal to me," Annie said.

Alice held up another Princessa box, this one smaller than the one that had held the bracelet, and gave it a little rattling shake. "They have matching earrings."

"Oh, all right!" Mary Beth held up her hands in surrender as the bell on the front door jingled again, and Peggy and Gwen came into the shop. "I'll give them a week."

"Give what a week?" Gwen asked as she put her knitting bag in her usual chair.

"Oooh, I love these. Look at the little tape measure." Peggy took the bracelet and draped it across her wrist. "Are you selling them, Alice?"

Alice shook her head. "Mary Beth is. Aren't they too cute? You know, Wally should get you one for your birthday next month."

"Good idea." Peggy admired the bracelet for a moment more and then passed it to Gwen. "I'll tell him to surprise me."

"Pretty," Gwen said, handing it back to Mary Beth. "But I'm dying to know more about your clock. I heard it was stolen from the repair shop. What did the police say? When do you have to go to court?"

"Looks like never, I'm afraid. The police released him after questioning because they have no evidence."

Mary Beth sat down in one of the cozy chairs, and the others joined her, Alice and Gwen and Peggy talking over each other, expressing varying degrees of surprise and outrage, and asking what had happened. By the time Mary Beth had explained the situation to them, they all had their projects out and had started working.

"Oh, but your beautiful clock!" Peggy pulled a length of red thread from her spool and snipped it off. "What are you going to do, Mary Beth?"

"I don't guess there's much I *can* do. Annie and I were talking about this before Alice came in. Whoever picked up the clock must have known my name and Annie's, and that the clock was at that particular shop."

"I don't know who that could be if it wasn't this Frank Sanders person." Alice squinted at the piece of pale blue linen she was cross-stitching, counting threads until she found the right place to start her next color. "But how did he know about the shop?"

"He definitely wasn't the one who picked up the clock," Mary Beth told her. "The police even checked that he really does have his own hair. The guy who took the clock was nearly bald."

"Frank Sanders would be too," Annie said, "if Mary Beth had her way."

Again the bell on the door jingled, and Stella came in.

"Sorry I'm a bit late. Jason had taken something apart in the engine, and it took him a little longer than he thought to get it running again so he could drive me here. What have I missed?"

Gwen sighed. "Mary Beth was just telling us that the police can't do anything about getting her clock back."

"I was afraid that might happen. It's a pity, Mary Beth, dear, and I'm sorry, but I'm not surprised." Stella sank into a chair and took her knitting from her bag. "It's not like they can post an officer to watch every petty thief twenty-four hours a day."

Alice squinted at her pattern and then took another stitch. "I wish there was something *we* could do. Some way we could make him tell us where the clock is. He must have it hidden somewhere."

"Well, he's not likely to just tell us if we ask nicely." Annie thought for a moment. "There has to be some way to make him show us where it is."

"Like that Sherlock Holmes story," Gwen said, "where he pretends the house is on fire to make the woman show where she's hidden the picture she's using for blackmail."

Annie tapped the arm of her chair with the tips of her fingers. "Except we wouldn't know what to set on fire."

"*Pretend* to set on fire," Gwen reminded her.

"Pretend to set on fire. We'd still have to have some idea where he has the clock before that kind of plan would work. But the basic idea is right. We have to figure out some way to make him give himself away." Annie shrugged. "Well, no need for us all to sit around all morning. Let's get back to work, and maybe one of us will think of something. All we have to do is figure out how to light a fire under Mr. Sanders."

$\sim 12 \sim$

*M*ary Beth carried her groceries into the house that evening, trying to keep from dropping anything. She always tried to carry too much at once, attempting to cut down on the number of trips from her car to the house. Invariably, it ended up being harder and took more time to keep everything balanced and intact than it would have if she had taken more trips with smaller loads.

She managed to get everything into the kitchen and was starting to put things away when the telephone rang. Why did people always have to call just as she got home? She decided to ignore the call, at least for the moment, and kept on putting frozen items into her freezer. The answering machine finally picked up, and she stopped for a moment, listening for the message that would follow the beep.

"Mary Beth, it's Melanie. I need you to call me right away."

Melanie again. And as usual, she sounded ticked off. She could wait.

"I told you not to bother Amy with your problems," Melanie continued. "I mean it. Call me!"

"All right. All right," Mary Beth muttered as she grabbed one of the grocery bags. "As usual, I don't know what you're talking about, but I'll call you. Give me just a minute."

She made the mistake of holding the bag at the top

rather than supporting it at the bottom. Before she got to the pantry, the paper tore through. Various cans of soup, fruit and vegetables thudded to the floor. A can of spaghetti sauce rolled until it bumped into the refrigerator and came to a stop.

She closed her eyes, forcing herself not to scream in frustration, when the telephone started ringing again.

"Listen, Mary Beth, I can't imagine why you think Amy should have to deal with—"

Mary Beth snatched up the phone. "What is it, Melanie? I just got home and haven't had a chance to even catch my breath. What exactly is going on?"

"I knew you were there." Her sister sounded pleased to be offended. "I'm too busy to play telephone tag with you. I'd appreciate it if you'd just answer your phone when I call. It's not like I just call up to chat."

"Heaven forbid."

There was a moment of silence.

"You know I'm very busy." Melanie's voice was frigid. "I certainly don't have time to keep calling you about this. I told you before to not bother Amy with your problems."

"I haven't bothered Amy with my problems. I've hardly had time to speak to her since the last time we talked about this. What's wrong now?"

"She's still badgering me about buying that building you're in and renting it out to you. Now she's even asking me to have some of our designers work on original patterns for crochet and knitwear for your shop to carry exclusively. It's a ridiculous idea, and I'd appreciate it if you'd stop putting this sort of thing into her head."

Mary Beth closed her eyes. It *would* be a brilliant idea. Melanie was certainly in a position to arrange that sort of thing, but Mary Beth would never expect it of her. "Listen, it's sweet of Amy to try to help me, but really, it's not necessary. I have someone who designs patterns for the shop already, and she does a fabulous job. I know you're busy, and I know you're not interested in investing in Stony Point or A Stitch in Time or having your name associated with it. Let me make it as clear as I can: I don't expect anything from you. You have your own business to run. I'll call Amy and tell her to leave you alone about this. Will that meet with your approval?"

"I already told her I wasn't doing anything of the kind. You don't need to call her. She thinks I'm a tyrant as it is."

Mary Beth fought the urge to rub in her own rapport with Amy. No need to dump gasoline on that fire. "What do you want me to do? I've already said I didn't ask her to talk to you about this. I can call her and tell her plainly that I'm not asking for anything from you and ask that she not discuss the matter with you again. Or I can refrain from calling her about it. I can't do both, and I can't do neither. Which would make you happy?"

Melanie fumed in silence for a moment.

"Do whatever you want," she said at last and hung up.

Mary Beth clicked off the telephone, and as much as she would have liked to hurl it across the room, she instead set it with a forced gentleness into the charger. The moment she did, it rang again.

I don't need more of this right now, Mel.

She let it ring twice more and then picked up.

"Hello?"

"Is this Mary Beth Brock?"

The voice on the other end of the line was female, very businesslike, and unknown to Mary Beth.

"Yes?"

"This is Officer Wiesner with the Brunswick Police Department. I'm calling regarding the charges you filed against Frank Sanders in the matter of your antique clock."

"Oh yes! Have you found out anything else? You haven't gotten the clock back, have you?"

"I'm sorry, no, and I don't want to get your hopes up at this point. I'm sure the officer who took your information told you it's fairly rare for us to recover this type of thing."

Mary Beth sighed. "Yes, he did."

"But there is one thing we'd like to ask you about. Can you come into the station sometime?"

"What is it?"

"We're hoping you can tell us that. It's just a piece of notepaper with some writing on it. We're not sure it has anything to do with the case at all, but we'd like to see if there's anything about it that you recognize."

"What kind of writing?"

"It's just a little poem, not very good, and some directions. Mr. Sanders claims it was something he made up himself. But, if you could come by and look it over, it might—"

"I'll be there first thing tomorrow."

*   *   *   *

"Come in! Come in!" Annie practically pulled Mary

Beth into the living room of Grey Gables and over to the sofa. "Sit down. Let me see it."

Mary Beth took a folded piece of paper out of her purse and spread it out on the coffee table. "It's just a copy they made for me at the police station. They said it's definitely in Sanders's handwriting. It was on his desk when they searched his place. The detective thought he was being a little funny about it, though Sanders claimed it wasn't anything. That's why they made a copy, for what it's worth."

Annie studied it for a moment:

I hide my face behind my hands,
But still my voice you hear,
And to the treasure of my heart
This path will lead you near

Stand between the trees,
face to the north, move west to east,
from the west move south to north
from the east move north to south
from the north move east again
from the south move downward
and then the key

"This first part's got to mean a clock," she said. "What else hides its face behind its hands and has a 'voice'?"

Mary Beth nodded. "That's what the police think, too, and that's why they were interested in it. But I don't know what the rest of it means, and they said they can't prove it wasn't Frank Sanders's bad attempt at blank verse."

Annie bit her lower lip, thinking. "Why would he write poetry about a clock anyway? I know he really liked yours, but that would be a little bit much, wouldn't it?"

She read the page over again, slowly this time, saying the words half under her breath. Then she froze.

"'And then the key.' Mary Beth, 'and then the key'! What if this is another clue from Geoffrey Whyte for Angeline?"

"But how—"

"Did you say the clock was something passed down from your great-great-grandmother along with the desk and the table?"

"Yes. And the vase that got broken too."

"Exactly. There was a clue in the table—the original clue. There was also one in the vase—the key with the lion on it."

Mary Beth nodded.

Annie picked up the paper from the coffee table. "Suppose the desk had this clue in it. That would explain why he was so interested in the clock."

"But there was nothing in the desk. And nothing in the clock. He almost took it apart when he was looking at it before."

"We *think* there was nothing in the desk. Remember that hidden cubby hole, 'the deeper secret place' in the desk? What if he found this clue in there? You said you didn't know about it, that your family didn't know about it. What if this was part of a clue Geoffrey Whyte put there in the 1860s and nobody ever knew it was there?"

Mary Beth exhaled heavily. "I don't know. By itself, this really doesn't mean much—just a silly rhyme and some directions. It does sound a little like a treasure hunt. Who knows what's at the end of it? Maybe Geoffrey left Angeline a love letter or an engagement ring. Maybe it was Confederate war bonds, and you know what they'd be worth by now."

"Yeah, next to nothing. But you're right. Frank Sanders wouldn't know about the clue we found or that this leads to anything of value. He wouldn't have risked jail time based on this by itself. There must be more. Either there was something else in the secret cubby, or he knows something about Geoffrey and Angeline that we don't." Annie leaned back into the couch cushions and frowned. "He's not likely to admit anything at this point, that's for sure."

"This clue talks about a key. Do you suppose he found a key hidden in the desk too?"

"He might have." Annie picked up the paper again, and her eyes narrowed. "I'd sure like to see the original of this. There may be a lot more to it that he didn't copy down. There has to be some way to find out what all he *does* know."

"Sounds pretty hopeless. The police say they won't be doing any more investigating unless I can come up with some new evidence against Sanders, and I sure don't know what that would be."

"We'll just have to think of something then, won't we?"

The corners of Mary Beth's mouth turned down. "I guess I just have to let it go. It was just an old clock, but I did love it. It was such a beautiful antique."

"And I was hoping we could solve Geoffrey's little puzzle too. Still, whatever it led to in the 1860s might be gone now. I'm sorry things have turned out so disappointingly for you lately." Annie glanced at her friend. "How are things going with Mr. Huggins? Is he still determined to sell out?"

"Still. He doesn't really have much choice at this point."

Mary Beth sighed. "I'm running out of time, and the Burly Boy people are really pressing him to sell to them. Poor man, he'd do a lot better to sell to them than take what he's asking me for the place. I just wish I had the money to do it. Actually, I wish he could keep the place and that his wife wasn't so bad off."

"I'll keep them in my prayers."

"They'll appreciate that."

Annie was silent for a minute, wracking her brains for some way to make Sanders reveal where he'd hidden the clock. The trees. There had to be trees out by the old Whyte place in Virginia.

"We're not going to give up quite yet," she assured Mary Beth. "As a matter of fact, I think, first thing tomorrow, I'll drop by the mayor's office for a few minutes."

"The mayor's office?" Mary Beth's forehead wrinkled. "Why the mayor's office?"

Annie grinned. "You'll have to trust me on that one."

~ 13 ~

The next morning Annie drove up Main Street and found a spot to park not far from Town Hall. After she got out of her car she took a moment to look down the charming street with its worn brick sidewalks and old-fashioned lamp posts. It was like a little piece of the past safely tucked away for everyone who lived in or visited Stony Point. She didn't want to lose it to so-called "progress." She *wasn't* going to lose it, if she had anything to say about it.

She walked across the street into the Town Square, a planned green space in the center of town which was crowned by a crisp red, white, and blue flag snapping in the sea-scented breeze. She made a beeline toward Town Hall, went inside and strode into the mayor's waiting room.

"Good morning, Mrs. Nash. How are you?" Annie asked Ian Butler's secretary.

"Fine, thank you, Mrs. Dawson. May I help you?"

Annie smiled. "I was hoping to see the mayor for just a moment."

"He's not busy right now. Go on in."

Annie walked over to the open door. Ian was seated at his desk, concentrating on something he was writing on a yellow notepad. He looked up when she knocked on the door frame, a sudden smile lighting his eyes.

"Well, if it isn't my favorite sleuth. How are you, Annie?"

He got to his feet and pulled up a chair for her. "I hope you didn't come over to talk about Burly Boy's Burgers again."

She returned his smile, feeling a little flush warm her face, and shut the door behind her. "I've been a real bear, haven't I?"

"Nah, not you. You love Stony Point, that's all. So do I. I still hope we're going to have some eleventh-hour miracle before it comes to tearing up buildings on Main Street to put in a fast-food place."

"I have an idea about something, Ian, and I need your help."

He lifted both eyebrows. "About stopping Burly Boy?"

"Maybe." She bit her lower lip. "Oh, I'm not sure. I don't know if this will help at all, even if it works, but I have to try. And I can't think of anything else."

His eyes were warm and understanding. "I'll be glad to help in any way I can. What do you need?"

"You have to do a lot of granting permits and such for people who want to build anywhere in Stony Point, don't you?" Annie asked.

"Well, I don't personally do it, but it's something the city does. Why?"

"How hard would it be to find out if someone is about to clear some land somewhere and is planning to start construction?"

He shrugged and shook his head vaguely. "I don't know. I suppose it would depend where it is."

"I guess what I'm asking is this: If you were to contact another town and ask for that kind of information, would they tell you?"

"It's usually public information. I guess you could call up the county clerk's office or the city clerk if it's an incorporated area. Is it someplace nearby?"

"Fairfax County, Virginia."

"Virginia?" He chuckled. "And what's all the way down there?"

She told him about Geoffrey Whyte and the clue about the trees.

Ian knit his brow. "How would you know whether these trees you're looking for are on a place about to be developed? And if they are, how would you know the right ones?"

The phone on his desk buzzed, and excusing himself, he picked it up.

"Yes, Mrs. Nash?" He nodded. "I see. No, I'll get it. Ask her to hold for just a minute." He put his hand over the receiver. "Speak of the devil."

Annie cringed. "Burly Boy?"

"Ms. McMillan herself. I guess I'd better take it. Do you mind?"

Annie grinned at him. "Do you mind if I listen in?"

He shook his head, chuckling. "Always the sleuth, aren't you? Sure, if you want to listen, go ahead. I'll even put her on speaker, if you'll stay out of the conversation."

"Ooooh, yes, please. I promise I won't make a peep."

Ian punched the flashing button on his phone. "Good morning, Ms. McMillan. How are you?"

"Pressed for time, Mr. Butler."

"Just so you'll know, I have a friend of mine here in the office with me," Ian said, glancing at Annie, "so our conversation won't be strictly private. Is that OK with you?"

"That's your call to make, Mr. Butler." The woman's words were cool and clipped. "I just wanted to let you know I've been on the telephone with Mr. Huggins about that Main Street property he owns. Due to the scheduling of some of our other construction projects, we'd like to get this one taken care of immediately. It will be some time before construction will start there, even if we can close very soon, but as you can well imagine, the timing on every project affects many of others."

"I can understand that, Ms. McMillan," Ian said. "How can I be of help?"

"Mr. Huggins has given one of his tenants an option to purchase, provided she can make the necessary financial arrangements by the end of next month."

"Yes, that is my understanding too."

Ms. McMillan laughed brusquely. "Let's be honest here, Mr. Butler. I've spoken to Ms. Brock. She has no reserves, no assets, and not even the vaguest prospect of obtaining any by the end of next month. You know that as well as I. *She* certainly knows it. And I'm quite sure Mr. Huggins knows it too."

"He might. I'm not sure what this has to do with—"

"As I told you, I've been trying to reason with Mr. Huggins about this. Of course, it's been very difficult having any sort of a detailed conversation with him. He's forever attending to something about his wife's treatment and then having to call me back."

Annie fumed at the thought of poor Mr. Huggins being badgered by this woman at such a difficult time, but she held her tongue.

Ian's usually genial expression was growing more and more stony. "He does have a lot of things on his mind right now, Ms. McMillan, as I'm sure you can understand. Anyway, I'm assuming there's a reason you've called me about this."

"Yes, of course." The woman's voice fairly crackled with disdain. "I suppose that, as the mayor, you have more than a little influence there in your little town. I thought you might be able to reason with Mr. Huggins and with Ms. Brock about this option and see if you could get them to agree to cancel it."

"And why would I want to do that, Ms. McMillan?"

"I think your town council was impressed with the numbers we gave them as far as what having one of our locations would do for your local economy. And of course, there are other community-enhancing efforts—literacy programs, green energy and conservation awareness, those sorts of things—which our corporation would bring to your area. It would obviously be in the best interest of Stony Point to get this deal done and as quickly as possible, don't you think?"

"Your company's presentation did impress the council, I'll agree, but Mr. Huggins and Ms. Brock's agreement is outside of their control—and mine too, for that matter."

"I understand that, of course. But you still have influence, Mr. Butler, and that's what I'm talking about. Surely the two parties can be made to understand that, for the good of the community, they might want to reconsider."

"So you want me to lean on them a little, is that it?"

Ian looked at Annie, a flicker of amusement in his eyes.

She put her hands on her hips and glared at the telephone.

"To put it plainly," Ms. McMillan answered, "yes."

Ian sat up in his chair and tented his fingers together on the desk in front of him. "I'm just curious, Ms. McMillan. Why is this so important to you?"

"I don't know what you mean. I told you we have to schedule these things out in advance. If I can get this deal done, I can move on to something else. Surely that's not too hard to understand."

"But is little Stony Point really worth all this trouble? I mean, there are places up and down the highway you could get."

For a moment there was only a cold silence.

"Mr. Butler, a lot of people from SLR & FFH have researched this particular location. We've done studies and marketing research and cost analyses. We've had a preliminary survey and inspection of the property. Based on all that, I have assured our CEO that this is the best place to open a location in the area. I have always gotten the locations I propose, and I'm not planning on letting this be the first one to get away. Even if we do have to wait out this ridiculous little option period between Huggins and Brock, I mean for this deal to go through. Either you can help me or you can't. Which is it?"

Annie and Ian exchanged incredulous glances.

Ian cleared his throat. "I don't think I can help you, Ms. McMillan. Mr. Huggins and Ms. Brock have an agreement that's good through the end of next month. I know you've spoken to both of them about terminating that agreement so you can go ahead with your project now, but it seems neither of them is interested in doing so, am I right?"

"Isn't that what I just said?"

Annie stifled a snicker at the increasing irritation in the woman's voice, and Ian put one cautioning finger to his lips.

"These people are my friends, Ms. McMillan. Both of them are dealing with difficult personal situations right now, and I don't think either of them needs me to turn up the pressure. Especially since I should be trying to make things easier for them."

"Oh please, Mr. Butler, this is a business matter, not a personal one. Your friendship with any resident of your town shouldn't have any bearing on the decisions you make as mayor."

"Forgive me, but I don't believe that's true. At least it's not true here in Stony Point. I'm not going to show favoritism to my particular friends, no—but I consider showing consideration to all of our residents a major part of my job." Ian's brown eyes flashed. "Now, is there something else I can help you with today, Ms. McMillan?"

"You realize that SLR & FFH has a lot to offer a small town like Stony Point. If you were willing to cooperate with us, we could be very generous."

Annie's eyes widened. Was she offering him a bribe?

Ian only chuckled. "I appreciate your community spirit, Ms. McMillan, believe me, but I really can't do anything to help you in this situation. Generosity of any kind isn't going to make the slightest bit of difference."

"I see." She sniffled audibly and disdainfully. "In that case, I suppose all I can do is wish you a good morning."

"You have a good morning too."

Ian hung up the phone, and Annie clasped her hands together.

"Oh Ian, I could just kiss you."

His face turned a little red, and he gave her an endearing "Aw, shucks!" look. "Just doing my job," he said, looking quickly at the floor.

Annie blushed too, realizing what she had just said, and he glanced up and gave her a wink.

"I'm not surprised Mary Beth didn't like her," Annie said, her smile fading. "Do you think she was trying to bribe you?"

Ian shrugged. "Hard to say. Sometimes people put out little feelers to see how you'll react. I always find it best to stop that kind of thing before it gets started. Whether or not that's where she was going, she knows where I stand. That's never a bad thing."

"You handled her just right. I'm amazed she keeps her job, treating people like that."

"I expect she's very successful at what she does, as long as you measure success strictly as getting what you want no matter what."

"Ah ... well, speaking of getting what we want ..."

She gave him a significant glance, and he laughed.

"Oh yeah. You didn't come here just to witness my masterful way of dealing with difficult people, did you? I take it you want me to find out what you want to know about land- clearing plans in Virginia—right?"

"It would be *very* helpful of you. And maybe—being the important person you are—you could find out quicker than just little old ordinary me."

"But that brings us back to the same question I asked before. How are you going to know which trees are the right ones or even that they're clearing the property where these trees are located? I mean, that sounds like a long shot to me."

Annie smiled at him. "You just find out what I need to know and leave the rest to me. I can't promise you it will solve the Burly Boy problem, but just maybe it will get Mary Beth's clock back for her."

*   *   *   *

Very late that afternoon, Annie's telephone rang. She stuck an envelope in the book she was reading, marking her page, and picked up the receiver.

"Hello?"

The voice on the other end of the line whispered something unintelligible. It was a man's voice, low and gruff.

"Hello?" Annie forced her voice to be strong and steady. "Who is this?"

"Seven owls fly low at midnight," he repeated a little louder.

"Ian! You scared me half to death. What in the world are you talking about?"

He laughed. "Didn't mean to scare you. I just thought if I was going to pass on classified information, I'd better use a password."

"Very funny. Next time, try not to sound like some anonymous weirdo. Now, tell me about this classified information. From Virginia?"

"Yep."

"Hang on while I get a pencil and paper. I want to make sure I don't forget anything."

"I don't know how this will help," Ian said, "but here goes. There are actually three places being cleared starting this week. All of them within fifteen miles of the old Whyte home." He gave her the specifics. "That last one is starting the day after tomorrow."

"Oh perfect. I want to get this done quickly, before our Mr. Sanders has time to figure things out."

"Umm ..."

Annie waited, smiling a little at his sudden uncertainty. "Yes, Ian?"

"You feel like having dinner sometime?"

She managed not to giggle. "I usually do most evenings."

"I mean with me."

He was so cute.

"When did you have in mind?" she asked.

"Umm . . . Friday night?"

"I think I can just pencil you in, Mr. Mayor."

"That would be great." She could hear the smile in his voice. "Seven?"

"Perfect," she agreed.

"And this stuff about the trees ..."

"Yes?"

"I still don't see how this is going to help anything, Annie. The information I got doesn't really tell us anything about particular trees or what they might lead the way to."

"Don't you worry about that, Mr. Mayor. You just hold

Burly Boy off for a little while longer, and let me get the rest of my plan set up. Thanks for your help."

"No problem, Annie. You know I'm always glad to help. Let me know if there's anything else I can do for you. Otherwise, I'll see you when I pick you up at seven on Friday night."

Ian hung up, and as soon as she heard the dial tone, Annie called Mary Beth.

"Hey there. It's Annie. Didn't you tell me Mandy Culbertson has been helping you out at the shop lately?"

"Oh yes. I told her she didn't have to. I mean her parents' insurance paid for everything. It was pretty upsetting at the time, but at this point everything is back to normal and no real harm done. But she's insisted on doing more, and I have to admit she's been nice to have around."

"Still, it's great to have Kate back at the shop too," Annie admitted.

Mary Beth sighed happily. "It certainly is. Between her and Mandy, the shop has never been so clean and well organized."

"Do you think Mandy might be willing to help get your clock back?"

Mary Beth didn't say anything for a moment. "What did you have in mind? I mean, she's just sixteen. I wouldn't want to put her in the middle of any kind of trouble."

"No, no, nothing like that. Just a little acting job. What do you think? Would she do it?"

Mary Beth chuckled. "I guess it wouldn't hurt to ask."

— 14 —

*I*t had been a slow business day, a day full of customers who hemmed and hawed, and took a lot of time but didn't buy anything, a tedious, never-ending day, and Frank Sanders was more than glad to see the end of it. He was just about to lock the front door when the telephone rang.

"Antiques and Oddities."

"Is this Mr. Sanders?"

The voice was vaguely familiar, but he couldn't quite place it. "Yes, it is. How may I help you?"

"Mr. Sanders, this is Annie Dawson. I ... uh ... I'm sure you remember me from the other day."

His professional cheerfulness vanished. "Yes, Mrs. Dawson, I remember you. Thanks to you and the local police, I've had a busy week."

Annie Dawson laughed a little. *Embarrassed, no doubt,* Sanders thought.

"I'm really, really sorry about that. I was so upset that day. I guess I just wanted to blame someone. My late husband always told me I should cool down and think things through before I did anything foolish. I know I should have listened."

"Yeah, maybe. Is there something I can help you with?"

"I'm sure you already know this, but the police have made it absolutely clear that they didn't find any evidence you were involved with the theft of my friend's clock. You have to admit it was quite a coincidence that it disappeared right after you were at Mary Beth's, but sometimes those things happen."

He didn't say anything. He just waited for her to say whatever it was she was trying to say.

"Anyway, I just wanted to apologize for all the trouble you've been through."

He smiled to himself, glad she couldn't see his face over the telephone. "Well, as you say, those things happen. Yes, it was a pretty unlikely coincidence. And—all in all—there was no real harm done. If they don't recover the clock, I hope the insurance will make good the loss."

"I think the insurance at the repair shop will eventually cover it. We're waiting to see."

"Well, then, it seems everything has been taken care of. I appreciate the apology, and really, don't give it another thought."

"That is very kind of you."

"Think nothing of it. Now, if there's nothing else … ?"

Again the woman laughed nervously. "Just one other thing. It's not a big deal, but I was hoping you might be able to help me."

"I suppose I can try. What is it?"

"Mary Beth told me that while you were at her house examining the clock you took several pictures. If you wouldn't mind, I was wondering if you could email them to me."

"Pictures?"

He *had* taken several while he was there—good clear photos of the fine detail work on the clock. Why would she be interested now?

"Yes. She said you had a camera—a digital one, wasn't it? They almost always are these days."

"Ah …yes it was."

"Then could you email the pictures to me? And I'd be very grateful if you could do it right away. Tonight."

"I'm sorry, but they're all gone."

"Gone? All of them? Oh no. Are you absolutely sure?"

"I'm afraid so."

"And they can't be recovered somehow? It would mean so much to Mary Beth to at least have some photographs if she doesn't get the clock back."

Sanders made a few silent taps on his keyboard and opened the first of the pictures he had taken, a detail of the clock face. Just what did they want with pictures? And why did they want them right now?

"No, I'm sorry. I would have liked to keep them. It was a beautiful piece, and I wanted to find out more about whoever made it. But my camera had a meltdown. It wasn't much of a camera anyway. It's in some landfill by now, I suppose."

For a very long moment, there was only silence from the other end of the line.

"Mrs. Dawson?"

"I'm sorry. I just—I really was hoping Mary Beth would at least have those pictures."

"I wish I could help." *No,* he thought, *I wish I knew what you were up to. Why the rush all of a sudden?*

"Thank you anyway, Mr. Sanders. And, again, I'm sorry about the trouble I caused you. I'll try to remember my husband's advice in the future."

He made his voice cheerful and pleasant. "You do that, Mrs. Dawson. Good night."

As soon as he hung up the phone, Sanders sat down at his desk and leaned close to his computer screen, clicking through the pictures he had taken of the clock—the face, the carvings, the works. What was it? And what had that woman suddenly figured out?

*   *   *   *

Once she had closed up A Stitch in Time for the day, Mary Beth hurried home. She had had another exasperating discussion with that pushy McMillan woman about agreeing to let them go ahead and buy the building.

Not quite yet, Ms. Burly Boy, she thought. *My time's not up until the end of next month, and I'm going to hold on until the last second.*

Mary Beth pulled into her garage and sat there for a moment, eyes closed. She was running out of time, and she knew it. Something had to happen quickly, something that would either make it possible for her to buy the building or make it clear what she ought to do instead. She needed a miracle of some kind, but so far she'd seen no answers to her prayers.

She didn't see any way she would ever be able to afford to buy the shop, especially if she had to buy the theater too. Yet every time she looked at other properties she might move to once it was sold, every time she even thought about going to look, she didn't feel right about it.

Wait, something inside her said. *Exercise some patience.*

When she went inside, she flipped through the bills and ads that had come in the mail and found a card from Amy in with them. It was just a sweet "thinking of you" card, and she immediately dialed Amy's number. Talking to her niece would be a bright spot in an otherwise difficult day.

"Auntie Beth! How great to hear from you. How are you?"

"I'm fine, sweetie. I just had a minute and thought I'd call you up. What have you been doing today?"

"You called to talk about Mother, didn't you?"

"Um ... no, actually. I called to say thank you for your sweet card and to see how you are. What's going on with your mother?"

"She just got through lecturing me about you."

"I'm sorry, honey. What did she say?"

"Just that you're old enough to solve your own problems, and that I should let you."

Mary Beth chuckled. "She's right, you know. I've been on my own, and I've been running a business by myself for quite a while now. I'll be all right."

"I know, and I'm not saying you're not capable or any-thing like that, but everybody needs a little help from time to time—especially these days. What's a family for?"

"The best help you can give me is to keep me in your prayers—OK?"

"I do that anyway." Amy sighed. "But what good does it do to pray about something if you're not willing to *do* something to help too?"

"Well, sometimes it's hard to know what to do or how much to do and when to do it. Sometimes it's best for a person to work her own way out of her troubles, as much as you hate seeing her struggle. We never know how much we can do if we don't get the chance to try."

"I know. But sometimes just a little help will get somebody through a bad time so she doesn't lose everything she's worked for her whole life."

Mary Beth wanted to hug her. "You're the sweetest person in the whole world, Amy," she said, a catch in her voice. "I love you more than anything for being the kind of person who would want to help."

"I wanted to use some of Grandma's trust money to help you, but I know Mother wouldn't agree, and she's the trustee until I'm forty."

"Oh dear, don't do that. I would never want you to do that in the first place, and your mother would have a fit if you even mentioned it."

"I know."

"And sweetie, you've got to stop asking her to help me too. It only makes things worse between us."

"But she *ought* to help you. She can afford it."

"But that's her money, not mine. It doesn't matter if she *can* afford it. She works hard for what she earns, and she should do what she wants with it. Besides, do you really know what she can and can't afford?"

"Well, she spends enough, I know that."

Again Mary Beth chuckled. "She does like the good life, I'll admit it, but it's still her money. If you don't give because you want to, you might as well not give. The scripture says that God loves a *cheerful* giver, not one who is badgered into doing it. And really, honey, I don't expect her to bail me out.

I've made my own decisions, even the ones that were mistakes. I like what I do, and where I live. I wouldn't like having all the pressure she has in the kind of business she's in. She has to always be worrying about the next new thing and making sure she's in with all the right people and that she's seen at all the right places. I would hate that. You know I would."

"I would too," Amy admitted.

"She does it because she likes it, but it's still not an easy life. I don't begrudge her what she has. I just want us all to get along. We're family."

"Why *can't* we, Auntie Beth?" There was pain in Amy's voice. "Why can't we all just do things together and have some fun? I can't even mention that I talked to you without her getting mad at me. I love you both. Why should I have to choose?"

"You shouldn't have to, honey. We shouldn't put you in the position where you feel like you have to. We're supposed to be the grown-ups here."

"I'm supposed to be a grown-up too, remember?"

"I don't care if you're thirty-nine or sixty-nine, sweetie. You'll always be my little girl. Anyway, we're *all* supposed to be mature, even if we don't act like it."

"*Mom* doesn't act like it, you mean."

"Don't blame her for everything, honey. I don't always try to be a peacemaker either."

Amy sniffed. "I don't know why she has to be mean to you, just because you're nice to me."

"She doesn't like sharing you, I expect."

"Yeah, right. It's not like she spends time with me or anything."

"But you're her daughter, not mine."

"But you're the one who really cares about me." Amy's voice broke. "You would never do things to hurt me just so you wouldn't be embarrassed in front of your friends."

"Sometimes, honey, what people try to do to make things better only makes them worse." Mary Beth's tears welled up at the sound of her niece's pain. "Your mother always means to do the best she can for you."

"Instead, I have to live my whole life wondering why my mother never understood how much I loved Cagney," Amy said. "And I wonder what my life would have been like if he had lived. She acted as if it was no big deal that I watched him be murdered."

Mary Beth's tears spilled down her cheeks, her heart breaking all over again to think of the horror of what Amy went through at the tender age of sixteen. Even though that was more than half her lifetime ago, Amy still lived with the pain. So did Mary Beth. Melanie's callous attitude toward Amy's situation had left her daughter with a never-healing wound and the two of them with a broken relationship.

"You ought to talk to your mother about it, honey."

"I can't talk to her about it." Amy's voice trembled. "She'll only tell me not to make a big deal about it. I can't take that from her again."

"I'm so sorry it's been like that between you, but you know it won't get better if you stop trying. You need to forgive her, and you need to forgive yourself. You'll never be close to your mother with all that hurt standing between you."

Amy drew a trembling breath, and then she laughed faintly. "I don't know how we got on that subject again. It's old news, and I know that's not what you called about."

"Amy, sweetie—"

"Anyway, I won't tell Mother any more of my big ideas, if that's what you want. I still think she ought to help you. I would do it myself if there was anything I could do. The money Grandma left me—"

"Is *yours*, honey. That's why Grandma left it to you. She left me some things too—things that I love. More than I need. Now I want you to stop worrying about me. I promise you I'll be fine. Now you tell me how your day went. How's that Everett of yours?"

"Oh, he's fine. We went to see *Les Miserables*, off-Broadway, and it was really good, even though we've both seen it several times before. Then he took me to this little Italian place for dinner. The tiramisu was divine."

"Ooh, and was this a special occasion?"

Amy giggled. "No. He said it was just because."

"Ah, you'd better hold on to a guy like that. And how's his little boy?"

"Peter's a sweetheart. We took him to the zoo a couple of weeks ago. He especially loves the tigers. Everett is thinking about getting him a kitten—tiger-striped, of course."

Mary Beth laughed. "Of course. Oh Amy, your mother is missing so much. All the little everyday things. Do you ever talk to her like this?"

"Not really. She doesn't have time for trivia."

"When was the last time you tried?"

Amy was quiet for a moment. "Years, I guess. Ever since I realized she wasn't really listening."

"Will you do something for me?"

"I know. You want me to call her up and talk."

"Could you, Amy? Just give it a try? Nothing serious. Nothing hard. Put all the difficult issues aside for a while and just have a nice talk."

"But ... what would we talk about? I mean, I don't have any particular news for her. I don't need anything. Life's just been going on as usual. What would I say?"

"I don't know, honey. Ask her about her trip to Milan, or what new lines she's working on, or how she's feeling. It doesn't matter. Just let her know you want to connect with her again. Tell *her* about Everett taking you to *Les Miserables*, and about going to the zoo. Let her know you want things to be better than they have been." Mary Beth paused. Maybe she'd stepped too far now. "You *do* want things to be better, don't you?"

"Yeah." Amy's voice was just a little more than a whisper. "Yes, I do."

"Maybe we both can take some little steps that will improve things. And if she's not interested, at least we don't have to feel bad for not trying, right?"

"Right."

"Don't do it if you don't feel like you're ready, honey. It's just something to think about." Mary Beth put a smile into her voice. "Now, tell me all about *Les Miz*."

— 15 —

Frank Sanders heard the shop's front door open and shut, and the telltale chatter of two young women. Customers. He let them look around for a minute and then came around to their side of the display shelves. They were just girls really. The younger of the two, the one with the long blond ponytail, was giggling and texting furiously on her hot-pink cellphone. The other girl was looking around the shop as if she were hunting for something in particular.

"Good afternoon, ladies. Is there something I can help you with?" He paused, thinking for a moment. He'd seen the older girl before. He couldn't place her for a minute, and then it came to him. "You were in here two weeks ago with Mrs. Dawson, weren't you?"

"That's right. We came in so I could look for something for my mom's birthday."

His smile hardened. "You mean, so she could grill me about that clock that was stolen from her friend."

The girl smirked. "Yeah, I guess that was the main reason. I do still need to get something for my mother though, and we didn't stay long enough for me to really have a chance to look around. You have some pretty awesome stuff here. My name is Jennifer, by the way."

He gave her the most suave of his smiles. "You don't

think I took that clock, do you, Jennifer?"

"No, though it's funny you should ask, because I work at the repair shop it was taken from," Jennifer said. "Mr. Malcolm's in Brunswick. Have you ever been there?"

"No." He shook his head thoughtfully. "No, I don't believe I ever have."

"Well, Mrs. Dawson brought me here to see if you were the one who picked the clock up. I never even saw her before that day. And of course, I had to tell her you weren't the guy, because you weren't."

He chuckled. "True enough. I'm glad you were able to help clear my name about that. Now how about this present for your mother. Just what kind—"

"Was Mrs. Dawson the lady who was asking you about the trees, Jennifer?" the blond-haired girl asked, overhearing the conversation. "I didn't understand why she'd call Mr. Malcolm asking about trees."

"Trees?" Sanders looked at the dark-haired girl. "Mrs. Dawson was asking about trees?"

Jennifer nodded. "It was the funniest thing. I don't mean funny like a joke, but funny strange, you know? Anyway, she called the shop asking if we ever took pictures of the clocks we fix. I thought it was a weird thing to ask."

He narrowed his eyes. "Did she say why she wanted to know? And what did that have to do with trees?"

"Yeah, it was really strange. I don't know what it was about the pictures. She thought the clock had some kind of code or something on it, and she said something about some trees that are going to be cut down in Virginia somewhere."

He forced a bemused laugh. "Trees in Virginia?"

"And a path," the blonde added, her ponytail bobbing as she nodded her head.

The other girl shrugged. "I didn't get it. She said she had to find the path before 'Angeline's trees' were gone. Sounded like she was in a big hurry too."

Again he forced a laugh, forced himself to sound only mildly interested despite his churning thoughts. "Did she say why?"

"I don't know. Just that they were about to start breaking ground for a mall or something out by some old white place. I didn't know if it was some people or some building or maybe the ground that was white."

The old Whyte place. What had that Dawson woman found out? Frank kept his expression pleasant, his tone conversational, impersonal. "Very odd. So *do* you take pictures of the clocks people bring in?"

"No. What for?" The girl looked at him as if he had lost his mind. "We wouldn't use them for anything. She said it probably wouldn't help anyway, because she really needed the real thing to take out there. Something about turning it to face north or something, and then knowing the path from that."

"Did she say anything else about the clock? Anything at all?"

Again the girl stared at him. "No. I don't know why she would ask us in the first place. Does any of that make any sense to you?"

"No, not at all." Sanders laughed, hoping he hadn't been too intense before. No need to make the girl suspicious. "I just think people are very interesting. I always like to try to figure out what makes them tick. Don't you?"

"Not really. I just—"

"You wouldn't mind figuring out what makes Robbie Harris tick, would you?" The blonde flashed her phone at the dark-haired one, giving her a glimpse of a text message. "Stacy says he asked about you."

"No way! What did he say?"

The dark girl tried to snatch the phone while the blonde shrieked with laughter and held it away from her.

Sanders felt his eyes glaze over, but he kept an indulgent smile plastered to his face until, after the giggles had turned to whispers and the whispers had finally stopped, Jennifer finally turned back to him.

"Sorry," she murmured.

"Not a problem."

"Anyway, I don't know what Mrs. Dawson was so urgent about. I mean, it was a very nice clock, and it was a family heirloom, but the shop's insurance will pay her friend back for it. It wasn't worth all that much."

"People are funny. Now, you wanted something for your mother's birthday, right?"

Neither of the girls bought anything, and as soon as they left the shop, Sanders hurried back to his desk. He rummaged through a glass bowl full of business cards until he found the one he wanted and dialed the number it displayed.

"Come on, come on," he muttered after four rings, and finally there was a click.

"Permits. This is Avery."

"Dave. How's it going? This is Frank Sanders."

"Hey, Frank. What's up?" Dave's tone changed from

businesslike to laid back. "You gonna let me fleece you again at poker on Saturday? Heh heh."

"Listen, do me a little favor, and I'll double that for you."

"Oh yeah?" Dave lowered his voice. "What's going on?"

"You guys ever do any work in Virginia? Fairfax County?"

"Yeah, some. Anything from Portland down to Charleston, we have people there, or I know somebody. What do you need?"

Frank smiled. "Just a little information, that's all. I just need to know if they're about to start clearing for construction on a mall or something like that near this house in Fairfax County." He gave Dave the location of the old Whyte place. "I'd say anything within ten or fifteen miles."

"That's all? Sure, I can find that out for you. I know a guy at the clerk's office over there. He'll know what's been approved." He chuckled. "I won't ask you why you want to know."

"Good idea."

"And that means you are gonna let me take you for some big bucks on Saturday, right?"

"Oh definitely. If you can find out what I want to know today."

"Today!" Dave laughed and swore softly. "What do you think I am, man? Houdini?"

"Gotta know today, Dave. Tomorrow may be too late."

"What exactly is going on here? This isn't going to get me in trouble, is it? I'm still not sure about that clock I picked up for you. I should never have let you talk me into that one."

"No, no, no. Look, all you have to do is find out where they're about to clear in that area. Maybe starting tomorrow. Maybe any time this week. Sometime really soon. That's all. Can you do it for me? What do you say?"

"I say it's a long shot for today, but I'll try."

"Trust me, I'll make it worth your while."

Just as he hung up the phone, Sanders heard the front door open and the chatter of several customers. Putting on his professional smile, he went out to greet them.

* * * *

Sanders picked up the telephone about half an hour later. "Antiques and Oddities."

"Frank? It's Dave. I think I found what you were looking for."

"That was quick. Hang on a second." Frank sat down and grabbed a pad and pencil. "OK, where is it?"

"Kind of in the middle of nowhere right now. They're clearing for a new housing development, about three miles off the main highway, a little more than five miles from the house you told me about."

Frank jotted down the directions Dave gave him. "And when are they clearing?"

"Day after tomorrow."

Frank laughed softly. So that was her hurry. She'd found where the trees were that the note talked about. Somehow he'd have to find them too. While they were still standing.

"Well thanks. I owe you, Dave. Big time."

Dave snickered. "You know this is all public information,

right? You could have called them direct."

"Yeah, but you know the right questions to ask and who to call to get past all the red tape. I owe you."

"Just bring plenty of cash on Saturday. Deal?"

"If this ends up being the right information, that won't be a problem."

Frank hung up the phone and went to his computer. As he expected, last-minute airfare anywhere was not inexpensive, but it would be worth it. He didn't have a choice at this point. He either went and found out what the Dawson woman was up to, or he missed out on the chance of a lifetime.

He clicked the final button to book his flight to Virginia and then locked the front door of the shop. It was a little early to flip the "Open" sign to "Closed," but he had some things to do before his flight left in the morning. He pulled the blinds shut and then, as an afterthought, taped up a little note card that could be read from outside the front door. *WE WILL BE CLOSED UNTIL SATURDAY. SORRY WE MISSED YOU.*

He recorded a similar message on the shop's answering machine. That should take care of things while he was away. If things went as he hoped, this little trip would be well worth missing a couple of days' sales.

He gave the front door a little tug, making sure it was firmly locked, and then he shut off the lights in the front part of the shop.

"Just one last thing."

He looked around the now-dim room as he walked toward the office area. It wouldn't be long before he had one of those posh shops like Park Cambridge, where they handled only the best of the best. And he would keep the very best of all of it for himself.

He'd miss his room full of treasures, the interesting bits of historical trivia that weren't worth much except as conversation pieces, but it wouldn't do to have a showroom like this in the better part of town. The posh set wouldn't like it. On the other hand, maybe in a day or two, he wouldn't have to care what anyone thought, posh or not.

He flipped off the light in the office and went into the warehouse, his steps echoing as he walked across the concrete floor to the loading dock. He locked those doors too. It wouldn't do to be seen. Not just now.

Once everything was secured, he took a sturdy cardboard box from the supply he kept and filled it halfway with packing peanuts. Then from one of the lower warehouse shelves, he slid a large wooden crate onto the floor. It was one of many marked with stickers and labels, some in Chinese, most in English. The labels on this particular crate showed an address in Hong Kong, one in New York, and the address of his shop. And several of them, in neon orange, announced that the contents were fragile.

He pried up the lid with the hammer he kept for just such purposes and propped the lid against the wall. Then he rummaged in the straw packing and took out a number of delicate porcelain dishes, small and dainty, in blue and white. He set those on the floor beside him and removed another layer of straw and lifted out a squarish object about fifteen inches high and ten inches wide wrapped in heavy paper. He set it on the floor beside him, careful not to jar it. Then he replaced the straw and the dishes and nailed the lid of the crate back into place. That done, he slid the crate onto the shelf once more.

He picked up the paper-wrapped object, laid it in the box he had prepared, and then covered it with more packing peanuts.

"That ought to ride just fine."

He tucked the box under one arm, and with a final glance around the tidy warehouse, flipped off the light and left through the back door.

— 16 —

"This is crazy."

"Just drive, Mary Beth." Annie leaned forward in her seat, silently urging Mary Beth's SUV to go faster. "You're going to lose him."

"He can't get far in this traffic. And if you're right, we know where he's going anyway. We should just let the police take care of it."

"They won't do anything." Alice leaned up from the backseat. "They don't have any evidence against him, and they more or less said they have more important things to do."

Annie scowled. "Well, if he is headed for the airport, that would be quite a coincidence, wouldn't it?"

Mary Beth pulled her SUV into the left lane, three cars behind the lime green compact Sanders was driving. "It's crazy, I tell you. Sitting outside his house all morning and then following him. We're not the police or FBI, you know."

"So we're private detectives," Alice said with a laugh.

Annie let her expression soften. "Maybe not detectives," she said, "but a trio of Jessica Fletchers."

Mary Beth pressed her lips together. "We really don't have any business doing this, you know. I can't believe I let the two of you talk me into it. We could get into all kinds of trouble taking the law into our own hands like this. After all, it's just a clock."

"No, I'm sure it's more than that, Mary Beth. There's something more in it, something Sanders knows about." Annie checked her watch. They still had plenty of time. "Besides, all we're going to do is watch him at a public place. He's headed south, so we still don't know if he's driving to the airport or to Virginia."

"I can't imagine he'd drive all the way to Virginia," Alice said, her brow knitted in thought, "not if he's trying to get there in a hurry."

"That's what I'm betting on," Annie said, nodding. "If he drives to Virginia, we're sunk, so if he doesn't turn off at the airport, then we'll just head back home, fair enough?"

"And if he does?" Mary Beth asked, clearly unconvinced.

Annie glanced first at Alice and then at Mary Beth. "Then we'll just see what happens. We're not going to do anything dangerous."

Mary Beth exhaled heavily, and no one said anything for the next few minutes. Sanders was still headed for the airport. At least that lime green car of his stood out in traffic. It was unlikely he would recognize any of them through the tinted windows of Mary Beth's SUV or think anyone was following him. Lots of people drove to the airport every day, didn't they? That is, if indeed, Sanders was headed for the airport.

Soon they were approaching the turnoff for Congress Street. If he were going to catch a flight, he'd have to turn now. The car's signal light flashed Sanders's intent to exit.

"He's got his blinker on. He's going." Alice leaned up from the backseat again, as much as her seatbelt would let her. "Don't lose him!"

Setting her mouth in a determined line, Mary Beth

pulled out of the left lane and worked her way through to the exit. They were five cars behind Sanders now.

"No, no, no," Annie muttered when a moving van blocked their view. "Do you see him, Alice?"

"No. Oh wait! There he is. He's pulled into the left lane again."

Mary Beth dutifully pulled into the left lane.

"No, don't do that," Alice told her. "It's too obvious."

With a sigh, Mary Beth put on her right blinker.

"No!" Annie and Alice said at the same time, and Mary Beth glanced at them, bewildered.

"You'll only make him notice you if you keep changing lanes. Just drive like you usually would. Don't do anything to attract attention." Annie gave her a steadying smile. "You're doing fine. Just keep on."

Sanders was only two cars ahead of them now, and Annie could see him fiddling with the radio, bobbing his head and tapping his fingers on the steering wheel, no doubt keeping time to the music. He seemed relaxed enough—smug even.

"You don't think he can see us, do you?" Mary Beth's eyes were wide, and her voice was barely above a whisper.

Annie shook her head. "I don't think so."

"And he certainly can't hear us," Alice added with a laugh.

Soon they were on International Parkway, heading for the parking areas of the Portland International Jetport. The lime green compact was still several cars ahead of them.

"What now?" Mary Beth asked.

Annie scanned the page of notepaper in her hand and then peered out at Sanders's car.

"I'm pretty sure he'll have to go on United. They have a flight at 2:20 that will get him to Dulles, and he'll have to rent a car to drive into Virginia. If that is his flight, we need Gate Eleven. If he's on a later flight, I don't think he would drive out here so early and just sit around the airport—not if he has your clock with him."

"He's pulling into the stack-up garage." Alice shaded her eyes. "We'll lose him if we take time to park."

Annie glanced at her list. "OK, we know where he has to go. Mary Beth, pull up to the terminal and let us out. Once you've parked, come over to the security checkpoint for Gate Eleven, but stay out of sight. Got it?"

"We'll lose him," Mary Beth protested.

"No. It'll take him a while to get parked and get his suitcase out. By the time he checks in, Alice and I will be watching for him. It's a good thing this isn't DFW though. We'd never find him."

"You're telling me. I've been through the Dallas/Fort Worth airport. It's like a major city all by itself." Alice stopped suddenly. "What if he checks his luggage in at the curb? Some airlines let you, you know."

"It doesn't matter. If he thinks that clock is valuable enough to steal, he's not going to let it out of his sight. It'll be in his carry-on. Don't you think so, Mary Beth?"

"I'm still not sure about this whole idea," Mary Beth said, a pained look on her face.

She pulled up to the terminal, and Annie and Alice hurried out. Annie was glad to find the terminal was just one long building for all the airlines. That meant there was only one for Frank Sanders to come through.

They took the escalator up to the security area and found seats near Gate Eleven. Sanders would have to come here to check in for Flight 3789, but they were—Annie hoped—too far away for Sanders to notice them.

"We have a good view from here." Annie sat down, scanning the crowd, trying not to get nervous. "When he shows up, we have to talk to him before he can check in. Once he's past that scanner, we can't get to him unless we buy tickets."

Alice fidgeted in her chair, looking around too. "I wish he'd hurry up. This is killing me."

In a few minutes, Mary Beth hurried up to them and sat down. For a long while, she merely clutched her purse, saying nothing. Then, finally, she bit her lip. "I can't do this."

"You don't have to do anything, Mary Beth." Annie gave her arm a reassuring pat. "Just stay over here out of the way. If there's trouble, get security."

Mary Beth nodded.

"OK, then," Annie said. "He's not violent."

"Just sneaky," Alice added with a giggle.

Annie giggled, too, and then her eyes widened. "Here he comes. Shh!"

Sanders was headed toward the check-in line, a small, hard-sided suitcase rolling along behind him.

"The clock has to be in there," Annie whispered. "It's the perfect size."

Sanders stopped at the end of the line. There were maybe a dozen people ahead of him, and he looked past them as he waited, not really seeing anyone, just passing the time until his turn came.

He certainly is a cool customer, Annie thought. Then she

swallowed hard. *Or maybe he really didn't have anything to do with the missing clock.*

No, it couldn't be that! It would be too much of a coincidence for him to be taking a trip to Virginia of all places and today of all days. Besides, the worst he could do is prove he didn't have the clock in his bag and go on his flight assured that she was truly out of her mind. He wouldn't press harassment charges against her, would he?

It was a risk she'd have to take.

She nodded reassuringly to Mary Beth and then motioned to Alice to follow her. They crept to the back of the line behind Sanders. Annie counted ten slow breaths and then moistened her lips and smiled.

"Mr. Sanders! It seems we're always running into each other."

He turned. She caught just an instant of panic in his eyes, and then the nearly suave smile replaced it.

"Well, if it isn't Mrs. Dawson. Again. You're not on this flight, are you?"

She shrugged, trying to look innocently nonchalant. "Virginia is a lovely state. And I always enjoy looking at the wild places, places where there are still open fields and flowers. ..." She smiled a little more. "... and trees."

He nodded. "Yeah. They're clearing out more and more places like that every day. I guess if we don't see them now, we'll never get the chance, eh? Well, enjoy your visit. I'm going to be at auctions all day. Still, it should be interesting. I love collecting rare old pieces."

"Even if they belong to someone else?

She narrowed her eyes at him, but still he smiled.

"Still making unfounded accusations, are we, Mrs. Dawson? I don't know what else I can do besides tell you I didn't have anything to do with the theft of your friend's clock. You've already been to the police with this, and they told you there isn't any evidence." His expression turned serious, and he moved almost imperceptibly closer. "I really don't want to have to tell the police you've been harassing me. That just wouldn't be very nice."

She lifted her chin. He was not going to make her step back. "Then why don't you call them right now? You can press charges against me, and then they can have a look inside that suitcase. How about that?"

He was pressing his lips together so hard they were white, but he gave her a tight smile. "I don't want any unpleasantness now. I have business to take care of, and at this point, I really find this all extremely boring. If you'll excuse me, the line is moving."

He turned and moved up about three feet closer to the check-in desk. She stayed right with him.

After a moment, he faced her again. "Don't make me have to make things unpleasant for you, Mrs. Dawson. I really don't want to cause you any trouble. You're a nice lady. Your friend's a nice lady. I'm sorry she lost her clock, but it has nothing to do with me. Can't you just leave me in peace?"

"I'm not doing anything but standing in line. It'll be interesting to see what those x-ray machines reveal. It's amazing what people try to carry onto planes with them."

His eyes darted toward where the screeners were staring at the monitors, sometimes stopping the conveyor belts that moved the carry-on luggage past the scans, sometimes asking passengers to open their bags for inspection. A little trickle of sweat ran down the side of his face.

"You realize they only let the screeners look at the monitors, don't you? The other passengers have to mind their own business."

"I suppose that's true. Still, sometimes one of the people screening the luggage is notified by the police to look for something in particular."

She gave a subtle nod to one of the screeners and then looked pointedly at Sanders. The screener acted like he hadn't noticed. Probably he hadn't. It didn't matter as long as Sanders didn't know that.

Another trickle of sweat ran down his neck and into his collar. He glanced at the check-in desk. Only one person ahead of him now and then the scanner.

Annie gave him her sweetest smile.

Finally he stepped up to the desk. The woman there smiled professionally and held out her hand.

"May I see your ticket, please, sir?"

Sanders looked at her, glanced at Annie, and then looked at her again.

"I ... uh ... I think I'm going to have to take a later flight."

He turned and grabbed hold of his bag. As he did, Mary Beth stepped into sight with a security guard beside her. Sanders's eyes widened, and he dodged to get around Annie.

But he didn't see Alice standing behind her. The two of them crashed together, the impact sending Alice reeling backward just as one of those airport service carts came zipping by, horn beeping.

"Alice!"

Annie yanked her back just before she would have been run over, but by then Sanders was half running down the corridor, his suitcase jolting behind him.

Alice was breathless but laughing.

"You were almost killed, and he's getting away," Annie scolded, wanting to hug her and shake her. "It's not funny!"

"Oh yes, it is."

Alice pointed, and Annie looked to see that Sanders's suitcase had burst open and he was scrambling to retrieve the contents scattered on the carpeted floor behind him. Mary Beth and her security guard were on him before he could even think of getting away.

Annie put one hand to her mouth, covering an incredulous smile. "But how—"

"I might have accidentally popped those catches open when he was talking to you." Alice looked sweetly heavenward. "Only accidentally, of course."

"You bad thing." Annie took her arm and leaned conspiratorially closer. "That was brilliant!"

They hurried over to where the other three were. The security guard was a burly man with a barbed-wire tattooed around his neck. The only hair on his entire head was in his sparse eyebrows and in the square inch of blond soul patch under his lower lip. Sanders didn't look like he was very interested in putting up a fight at this point.

"Is there a problem, sir?"

"I ... uh ... no. No problem." Sanders looked up at the

guard, smiling and sweating, trying to conceal a split-open cardboard box behind a bathrobe and a pair of pants. "I just had a little accident."

"You almost caused one." The guard crossed his beefy arms across his chest. "And this lady says you have something of hers in there."

Sanders's face turned red as he still tried to stuff everything back into his suitcase and kick aside the packing peanuts that had dribbled from the box. "That *lady*, as you call her, has had her friend here harassing me for days now. The police, if you'd care to check with them, have told them all that there is no evidence whatsoever that I have what they're looking for. Feel free to call them up if you like, but I'm late for an appointment. Excuse me, please."

The guard turned to Mary Beth. "Is this true?"

She glanced helplessly at Annie. "Well, I—"

"Of course it's not true." Annie put her hands on her hips and nodded towards the suitcase. "Isn't that your clock right there, Mary Beth?"

One corner of the clock was peeping out of what was left of the packing peanuts, exposing an exquisite carving of an oak tree. Sanders could only stand gaping as Mary Beth nodded.

"I'm sure it is. There can't be two of them like that."

The security guard eyed Sanders and the debris around him. "I think all of you had better come with me until we can get this all sorted out."

— 17 —

The guard picked up the clock. With it securely in one hand and Sanders's arm firmly in the other, he led them all through some doors marked "Private" and into a sitting area. Unlike the colorful seating and decor in the airport lounges, this place was strictly utilitarian. The gray walls were bare. The chairs were straight-backed, hard-plastic molded seats bolted to metal frames. They also were gray.

Besides the chairs, the only other furniture in the room was a gray metal desk that looked as if it had been repaired, painted, and passed down a number of times. The security guard sat down behind it and put the clock on top of it.

"Now, I want to know what's going on here. Do we need to get the police involved?"

"No!"

Mary Beth and Sanders both spoke at the same time, and then Sanders ducked his head.

"Go ahead and take it back," Sanders said. "I don't care any more. But you'd better catch your flight, however many of you are going. If you don't, what you're looking for will either be found or plowed under. I don't want the stupid clock."

The guard looked at Mary Beth. "Then that is yours, ma'am?"

"I'm sure it must be. Is it OK if I take the paper off?"

The guard nodded, and Mary Beth carefully unwrapped the clock.

"Yes, it's definitely mine." She gave Annie a worried look as she rubbed one hand over the glossy wood. "You don't think it's broken now, do you?"

"Don't worry," Annie said. "I'm sure Mr. Malcolm will be happy to check it over once we get it back. And I'm sure he won't let there be any mix-ups this time."

Sanders scowled. "Can I go now?"

Annie shook her head. "I want to know what you were after. What exactly did you think you were going to find?"

"Same thing as you." He narrowed his eyes at her. "Don't you think you'd better get out of here before you miss your plane?"

Annie and Alice exchanged grins.

"I wasn't planning on going anywhere but back home," Annie said.

"But the trees. I had it checked out myself. They're clearing that field starting tomorrow. Everything will be gone." He stopped, and then he laughed abruptly. "You don't know where it is any more than I do, do you?"

Annie responded only with an enigmatic smile.

"And those two girls at my shop were part of the scheme too." He looked as if he wanted to kick himself. "Great. That's just fabulous. Outwitted by Charlie's Angels' grandmas."

Annie pressed her lips together. "How about you tell us what you know about Geoffrey Whyte, and the clue you found? The police gave me a copy of the notes you had when they questioned you before. What do you think it means?"

He shrugged. "I don't know what you're talking about.

That was just some silly poetry I was playing with. It's very personal."

"Not as personal as going to jail," Alice said.

Sanders rolled his eyes. "Why should I tell you anything? Do what you want. Press charges. I'm not going to help you."

"But maybe we can help you." Annie glanced at Mary Beth. "If you were nice and told us everything you know and why you wanted the clock so badly, Ms. Brock may not find it necessary to press charges against you."

Sanders rolled his eyes. "For petty theft? I don't have any prior convictions or even any arrests. I probably won't get anything worse than probation."

"For petty theft, maybe. But for assault? Maybe even attempted murder?"

"Attempted murder? Hold on, now, Mrs. Dawson, you can't—"

"You pushed us right into the path of that luggage carrier. The security guard saw it all. Seems like a pretty deliberate attempt to kill me and my friend Alice, if you ask me."

Sanders snorted, "Don't be silly."

"You saw it all, didn't you?" Annie turned to the security guard. "If I hadn't pulled my friend out of the way, she could have been badly hurt."

The big man fixed Sanders with a baleful eye. "That was a pretty reckless thing to do, sir. Maybe it was and maybe it wasn't deliberate, but it was reckless, and you did put these ladies in danger. I'd have to testify to what I saw. It'd be wrong not to. And you've as good as admitted to taking this lady's property. I'd have to testify to that too."

He and the three women looked at Sanders, waiting for his response. For a while, he just sat there, his nostrils flaring and his lips twitching as he glared at them. Then he threw up his hands.

"All right. All right! It was a crazy thing to do. You know the Civil War period is a special interest of mine. A few years ago, I bid on some antique pieces from the Whyte estate. Part of the lot was a box of books, and one of those books was Geoffrey Whyte's diary. There wasn't much in it of note. He kept some detailed records of his expenses and sometimes commented on current events and parties he'd gone to. But that changed in 1861. He wrote about this girl he'd met, except he never used her name. He just said things like, 'A and I met at a supper party at J's' or 'Saw A at Mrs. B's barbecue, terribly fetching.' Later on, things evidently got serious between them, and he was worried about what would happen to her if he went to war and was killed. His mother, it seemed, held the purse strings still and disapproved of the girl. He seemed very upset that she found the girl not of a suitable class to consider marriageable and wouldn't give him even a portion of some inheritance he had due him from a deceased grandfather. The moment he was of age, he took all the money and bought something. I don't know what, but it was something he thought would provide for this girl in case he didn't come home from the war."

Annie narrowed her eyes at him. "It must have been something with intrinsic value," she said. "I don't know about right then, but at some point Confederate currency was notoriously unstable."

Sanders nodded. "He said he wanted something his

mother wouldn't find and demand the girl return, something 'A' could easily conceal. Something durable."

"What was it?"

"He never said anything specific in the diary. I tried to do a little nosing around, but I never could find out anything about it or even who 'A' was. He never wrote out her name in his diary. Maybe he didn't want Mother scaring her off."

Annie gave him a hint of a smile. "I understand Georgianna Flippin Whyte was quite a formidable woman in her day."

"Must have been. Geoffrey thought so at any rate." Sanders shrugged. "Anyway, I thought it was a great story, but I didn't think anything else about it until I bought that writing desk of hers." Sanders jerked his chin toward Mary Beth. "I couldn't believe it when I checked it out at Park Cambridge Antiques and found that clue in it."

"There was a key, too, wasn't there?"

He glanced at Annie, his mouth taut. "Maybe."

"Mr. Sanders, do you want these charges dropped or not?"

"OK, OK." He dug in his pocket and brought out a little key, small and brass like the others Geoffrey had left behind. "But I couldn't figure out what it goes to. There's nothing on the clock with a keyhole except where you wind it, and that's the wrong kind of key. The base of the clock is just a solid block of wood. And where are the trees he's talking about? If that place they're about to clear doesn't have anything to do with this—"

"And it doesn't," Annie said.

"—then where are the trees he's talking about? I've

been out to the old Whyte place, or what's left of it. If there were two specific trees he had in mind, I guess they're gone now. I thought there had to be another clue inside the clock that gave the right path to the trees he mentioned. I even thought there might be something in those carvings that would give me a path—some kind of directions to find the treasure—but I don't see it. I've studied that stupid clock until I'm cross-eyed and color blind, and I can't find the clue he's talking about." He tossed the key onto the table in front of her. "I suppose whatever he left is gone now too. I don't guess there's any reason for me to go to jail for something that's not there anymore."

Annie looked at Mary Beth. "Does that satisfy you?"

"What did you do to make my clock stop?" Mary Beth asked, her mouth taut.

Sanders shook his head. "Nothing. Why do you think that?"

Annie rolled her eyes. "So it just happened to stop right after you left that day?"

"Nothing I did on purpose anyway." He shrugged. "While I was examining it, I guess I could have turned the face a little, enough so the mechanism behind it wasn't hanging straight anymore. I've done it before winding my own clocks. It doesn't hurt anything, but it keeps the clock from running right."

"So you were the one who broke into my house."

"You said you weren't pressing charges."

"Not if you tell us the truth." Annie gave him a hard look. "It was you, wasn't it?"

"I didn't know the clock had stopped, so I didn't know

you'd taken it to be repaired. When I broke in and found it wasn't there anymore, I didn't want to take anything else. Nothing that the police would really bother to try to find."

Annie still glared at him. "And how did you find out where the clock was?"

He jerked his chin toward Mary Beth. "I heard her say you were taking the clock into Brunswick to be fixed. There's only one shop there that does work on specialty pieces like that. I just sent a friend of mine out there."

"And who's this friend? I suppose he's the one who actually picked up the clock while you were giving yourself an alibi in New York."

"Oh no, Mrs. Dawson, that's one name you won't be getting out of me. He thought he was just helping pull a prank on a friend and didn't even know he was breaking the law. He's not part of the deal."

"Then we don't have a deal."

"No." Mary Beth put one hand on Annie's arm. "It's all right. It's not like he has any reason to do this to anybody else. I have my clock back and the little bit of information we were missing. I guess that's the best we can hope for now. I don't think Mr. Sanders here will be trying any other criminal activities. The police will come down hard on him if any other complaints are brought against him, I'm sure."

Sanders gave her a half-smile, one that seemed surprisingly genuine. "Thank you, Ms. Brock. I'll make it up to you."

The security guard gave him a hard look, and then he turned to Annie and her friends.

"So is this settled?"

Annie fixed Sanders with a steely glare. "Did you

bring some cash to take on your trip today?"

"Yes, but I—"

"How much do you think it will cost to replace your CD and DVD players, Mary Beth?"

Mary Beth shrugged. "I don't know. They're not all that expensive these days. Not the ones I had anyway."

With a sigh, Sanders pulled out his wallet, took out several bills, and laid them on the table in front of Mary Beth. "Will that do?"

Annie gave the money a disdainful look. "And there was the window she had to have replaced."

Sanders briefly closed his eyes, and then he took the remainder of the bills in his wallet and added them to the others. Annie counted them out and gave them to Mary Beth.

"Does that cover everything, Mary Beth?"

Mary Beth nodded. "I can't think of anything else."

"OK," the security guard said. "Now is everybody happy? No need to call the police? I still can, you know."

"I think we're fine now," Annie told him. "You've been very helpful. Um ... in case our friend here changes his mind later on, you would be willing to testify about what happened today, right?"

"Yes, ma'am. I'd be happy to." He fished in his pocket, pulled out a much-handled business card and gave it to her. "If any of you ladies need me, you just call."

Annie glanced at the card and suppressed a giggle as she put it in her purse. He certainly didn't look like a Timmy Pertwee.

"Thank you," she said, offering him her hand. "Really,

you've been very helpful. Come on, girls—let's go home. Mr. Sanders, you'd better go see if you can get the money back for your ticket to Virginia. There's nothing there for you to see."

Sanders only gave her a sour look. "My ticket was nonrefundable."

— 18 —

Annie sighed as Mary Beth pulled onto the highway heading away from the airport and back toward Stony Point. "At least we got your clock back," Annie said.

"You don't sound very happy about that," Alice said.

Mary Beth smiled at Alice in the rearview mirror. "I am. Mr. Sanders is probably right. If there was some kind of treasure, it must be long gone by now. But I have my clock back. Whatever happens with the shop will just have to happen."

Annie chewed her lower lip, staring out the front window of the SUV, not really seeing anything. It was maddening. Geoffrey had to have left something for Angeline to find. Something valuable. What could it have been? And what had happened to it?

Sanders had known about the Whyte home, and he had checked the surrounding area. The trees Geoffrey had mentioned must have been someplace special to him and Angeline all those years ago. If they hadn't been cut down, there was no way of identifying them now, was there? *Between the trees.*

Annie cleared her throat. "Mary Beth?"

Mary Beth pulled into the right lane to let a faster car pass. "Hmmm?"

"Did you ever go to the house Angeline lived in? Maybe

the trees in the clue were on her land somewhere."

Mary Beth chuckled. "If they were, then we've really hit a dead end. I remember Mom telling me how upset her mother was when they tore that place down to build a highway sometime back in the thirties."

Annie exhaled heavily. "I don't suppose you ever heard of any special place around there? Some trysting place for young lovers?"

This time Mary Beth laughed outright. "Just how old do you think I am? And I never lived in the area myself, you know. But, no, I never heard Mom or Grandma talk about anything like that."

"You'll just have to give this one up," Alice said. "Take yourself out of crime-solving mode, and put yourself back into enjoying-a-normal-life mode."

"You're right. But I think if I'm not going to be in crime-solving mode, I need to be in figure-out-what-to-do-about-Burly-Boy mode. I guess I've been hoping that, whatever it was, what Geoffrey left for Angeline would somehow fix the Burly Boy situation too."

Mary Beth looked straight ahead, watching traffic, but Annie could see a flicker of sadness in her eyes.

"I guess I was hoping that too," Mary Beth said. "I suppose that would be too much of a miracle to ask for." She sighed and then abruptly straightened her shoulders and smiled. "But it was a good way to keep my mind off things I can't do anything about."

Alice grinned. "It was fun, wasn't it?"

"It's only fun when you can actually solve the puzzle," Annie groused.

"Now, now," Alice said, shaking her finger. "Burly-Boy mode, remember?"

* * * *

For the next couple of days, Annie went through her usual routine with half of her mind focused on her normal daily tasks and half if it sifting through different ways she might help Mary Beth save A Stitch in Time. Everything—it seemed—was either impractical or impossible. Finally she went across the lawn to the carriage house and knocked on the door.

There was no answer. Alice was probably giving one of her jewelry parties. Or was it Divine Décor this time?

With a sigh, Annie turned to go back home. Before she reached her own door, Alice's red Mustang turned into her driveway.

"Hey. Were you looking for me?"

Annie waved and scurried over to the car. "I was thinking maybe you and I should go over to Mary Beth's and do some brainstorming. What do you think?"

"I think you're nuts," Alice said with a good natured shake of her head, "but if Mary Beth is willing to have a little company, I'm game. As long as the conversation in no way turns to anything concerning the selling of costume jewelry. I've had my fill for the day."

Annie laughed. "Let me call Mary Beth and see if she'll let us stop by, and then I'll grab my purse and be right out."

Annie hurried inside and punched in a telephone number. Mary Beth picked up before it even rang.

"That was quick."

"Annie? I was trying to call you."

They both laughed.

"Listen, Mary Beth, Alice and I thought that, if you're up to it, we'd come by your place and brainstorm about the Burly Boy problem."

"Ugh. I don't know if my brain will go there anymore. But, yeah, come on over. I have something for you to see."

"Ooh, what?"

"Uh-uh. You'll just have to come and see."

* * * *

Alice's Mustang got her and Annie to Mary Beth's in record time, and Mary Beth was standing at the door waiting for them.

"You won't believe what I got in the mail today. Come in, you two, and sit down. Coffee?"

Alice and Annie followed her into the kitchen and sat at the table.

"So what did you get? Did Burly Boy decide to build somewhere else?"

Mary Beth frowned. "No, that's still on, I'm afraid. Mr. Huggins hasn't signed the papers yet, but my time is about up, and I don't have any more alternatives."

"I'm sorry, Mary Beth," Annie murmured. "I wish there was something we could do."

"It's OK. That's not why I called you over here anyway. I thought you'd like to see this."

She put a letter down on the table in front of them.

Ms. Brock—

I thought you'd want this. I'm sorry it's not really worth anything except as a little family history. Thanks again.

Alice snatched up the paper. "It's signed Frank Sanders. Well."

"Wait a minute. You didn't let me read the P.S." Annie took the letter from her. "'I told you I'd make it up to you.' What does that mean? What was in the letter?"

Mary Beth opened a notebook and brought out another letter, this one very old and yellowed. Annie recognized the writing at once.

"That's from Geoffrey."

Her eyes sparkling, Mary Beth nodded. "It was hidden in that secret cubby hole all these years, and we never even knew it. I'm glad Mr. Sanders was good enough to send it back to me. I think it belongs with Angeline's dance card and her other memories of Geoffrey."

Annie strained to read the faded ink.

Sweetheart,

I fear I do not have good news for you. I spoke to Mother regarding the legacy left me by my Grandfather Whyte. She still refuses to grant me any part of it until I come of legal age. Four months is not so long, my darling, but I cannot bear the thought of leaving you alone and unprotected should the war well and truly come to pass.

If only Mother knew you. She would love you, as anyone who knows you must. For the present, however, I will find some way to provide for you that she will not know of.

Be patient.

Yours with all my heart,

Geoffrey

Below that, still in Geoffrey's handwriting, was the original of the clues Sanders had copied down to carry around
with him:

Stand between the trees,
face to the north, move west to east
from the west move south to north
from the south move east to west
from the east move north to south
from the north move east again
from the south move downward
and then the key ...

Just as she finished reading, Annie heard four delicate
chimes from the direction of the mantelpiece—from Mary
Beth's antique clock.

"I didn't know it chimed," Annie said, enchanted by the
angelic tinkling of the bell.

Mary Beth laughed. "After all this time, I didn't know
it either. Isn't it beautiful? Your Mr. Malcolm did wonders
with it, and after it had been silent for so long."

"Well, that's a treasure in itself," Alice said. "Though it's
too bad we couldn't find what Geoffrey left behind."

Mary Beth sighed. "I'm sure Mr. Sanders searched all
over this clock looking for another clue. And Mr. Malcolm
would have taken it all apart when he was fixing it. There's
just nothing here anymore. Maybe it's not even the right
clock."

Annie stood staring, seeing but not seeing the clock
before her. "Between the trees. Between the trees! Oh my
goodness, I can't believe how stupid I've been!" She turned
the clock around. "What are those?"

Mary Beth wrinkled her forehead. "They're trees, but you can't really stand between them, can you?"

"No, think about it." Annie turned the clock back around the right way and tapped the glass on the front. "What is this?"

"The face, but—"

Annie took the clock off the mantel and set it down on the end table. "If I stand 'between the trees' like this ..." She stood behind the clock. "... and if I assume the face is facing north, then what happens if I follow these directions?"

Alice laughed. "And do what? Wander around the way it says until an amazing treasure magically appears? There's nothing in there."

"I don't know, but I want to try something." Annie put both hands on the base of the clock. "Read me the first part."

Mary Beth picked up the paper and read: "Stand between the trees, face to the north, move west to east."

"OK, stop there. If the face is north, and I'm standing behind it, 'between the trees,' then west is to my left and east is to my right."

Annie pushed on the base of the clock, trying to slide the front from the left to the right. At first nothing happened, and then it budged a little. She pushed harder, and part of it moved to one side.

Mary Beth's mouth fell open. "Oh Annie."

Annie's hands trembled. "I wasn't sure it would work, but it was the last thing I could think of. I've seen those Chinese puzzle boxes. They look like they're just solid blocks of wood, but if you know the right pattern, you can open them up."

"Amazing," Alice breathed.

"Which way next, Mary Beth?" Annie asked.

"From the west move south to north."

Annie slid the left side of the clock base forward and then looked again to Mary Beth.

"From the south move east to west."

Annie pushed the backside of the base to her left. "And then?"

"From the east move north to south, and then from the north, move east again."

Annie pushed the right side of the base toward herself and then slid the front panel further to the right. "OK, and then what?"

"I can't stand it," Mary Beth said, her voice unsteady.

"What's next!" Alice insisted.

"All right already!" Mary Beth took a deep breath. "From the south move downward, and then the key."

Annie slid the back of the base down, exposing a tiny keyhole, and then she glanced up at both of them. "And then the key."

"Wait a minute." Mary Beth disappeared into her kitchen and then came back with the little brass key Sanders had turned over to her. "Here it is."

Annie stepped back from the clock. "Go ahead."

Alice's blue eyes sparkled. "Oh, come on. You're making me crazy."

Mary Beth turned the key until there was a little clicking sound and then she gave it a tug. The key and the whole backside of the clock base came away in her hand, exposing a small hollow space packed with cotton wadding.

"Goodness!" She pulled out several pieces, but there

was still more. "No wonder we thought this was a solid block of wood. Whatever's in here, if there's anything besides packing, certainly wouldn't rattle."

Annie felt one of the pieces of wadding. "It's almost like new, it's been protected from light and moisture for so long."

"At last!" Mary Beth had finally exposed the treasure Geoffrey had left for Angeline more than 150 years before. It sparkled at its first touch of light. "Oh my. Oh ... it's just ..."

She pulled on it, and out slid a glittering multistringed necklace of rubies, diamonds, and pearls set in gold.

"Ooh," Annie breathed.

For once, Alice was speechless.

Mary Beth shook her head. "That is ... it's ... I can't believe it."

"Is there anything else in there?" Annie asked. "You ought to check."

Mary Beth pulled out the rest of the cotton wadding, revealing a matching ring and earrings. All of the jewelry was in pristine condition, sparkling as if it had just been made.

She traced her finger over the ornate golden setting that held the necklace's largest ruby. "Do you think ... I mean, could they possibly be real?"

The three of them just sat staring for a very long time.

"I'm just—" Mary Beth caught her breath. "I'm so overwhelmed, my head's spinning."

Annie examined the jewels a little more closely. "I don't know what these are worth, but it has to be a lot. Surely it would be enough to buy your building."

"If they're real," Alice reminded her.

Mary Beth's expression sobered. "Wait a minute. If this was Geoffrey's and Angeline never got it, wouldn't it be part of his estate? Maybe I don't have any right to it at all, real or not."

"What do you mean?" Alice frowned. "It's been in your family for years, whether or not you knew about it. And obviously, he meant for her to have it. How could it not be yours?"

Annie thought for a minute. "I don't know. Even if it was legally hers, what about any other heirs? If Angeline was your great-great-grandmother, what about your great-aunts and -uncles? Or their heirs? The money from this might have to be spread out among a lot of people."

Mary Beth sat down, still staring at the sparkling jewelry. "I didn't think about that. I guess I'm right back where I started."

"Do you have a family tree written down anywhere?" Annie asked. "Maybe it would give you some idea about who you'd have to consider."

"Just the Bible. I think my grandmother kept birth and death records in it up to when Mom was born. I know Mom's only brother and sister died of diphtheria when they were children back in the 1930s. I'll have to look up the rest."

Mary Beth's family Bible was well read but in amazingly good condition for its age. Still, Annie took extra care when turning the fragile pages. The earliest marriage listed was that of Angeline's parents, John Morrow and Paralee Walling in 1837. Angeline was the third of their eleven children. Angeline and her husband, Mary Beth's great-great-grandfather James Parish, had only one daughter, Emma. Emma had one daughter and three sons, but all of the boys died in 1918.

"That was Mom's mother and her uncles," Mary Beth said when Annie asked about them. "Grandma said her brothers were all killed at the battle of Château-Thierry in World War I."

"None of them had children?" Alice asked.

"No. I think they were all very young."

"Then, really, it seems to me that whatever was left to Angeline would be passed down to you, Mary Beth." Annie smiled and handed the Bible back to her. "And you know Geoffrey intended the jewelry for her. I don't think you have to worry about being entitled to it."

There was worry in Alice's expression. "I don't know if Geoffrey's intentions are enough to give you good claim to the jewelry, Mary Beth. A letter vaguely talking about providing for Angeline isn't the same thing as a legal will."

"But he didn't have children when he died," Annie protested.

"No, but he would likely have had brothers or sisters who did. No, wait, didn't you say Geoffrey was the only son? Anyway, he may have had sisters, and it's their descendants who might have a claim. With something as valuable as that necklace, you'll have them crawling out from under rocks for a share of the money. And it might leave Mary Beth out entirely."

"But it's been in our family for a century and a half," Mary Beth protested, and then she sighed. "But I suppose, if someone else has the right to it, he might need it as badly as I do—or worse. And honestly, I don't want anything that really belongs to someone else."

"Obviously, this isn't going to be a simple matter to get cleared up." Annie smiled at Mary Beth. "I think you need to talk to an appraiser and a lawyer, and find out what you need to do next."

Alice picked up the necklace and held it up to her neck, admiring herself in the mirror over Mary Beth's couch. "This red doesn't really work with my hair, I suppose, but, ooh, isn't it pretty?"

Annie laughed. "That's not Princessa, you know. You'd better be careful with it."

"I don't think I want it in the house." Mary Beth took the necklace back. "If even one of those stones is real, it's worth a lot. I don't know what kind of trouble I'd be in if something happened to it now."

Annie checked her watch. "If we hurry, we can get to the bank before it closes. I'm sure they'd love to give you a safe-deposit box to keep that in until you can get it appraised and insured." She laughed suddenly. "If only Frank Sanders could see us now."

Mary Beth mouth turned up at the corners. "If only he had had all the pieces of the puzzle, he might have found the jewelry."

"I guess Geoffrey wanted to make sure his mother didn't know about Angeline," Annie said, "or her name would have been in his diary and other papers. Then Sanders might have found the treasure after all."

Mary Beth nodded. "I guess it helped that she didn't live near the Whyte place either. That might have made her easier to trace too."

Annie knit her brows. "She didn't?"

"Oh no. Didn't you say the Whytes were in Fairfax County? That side of our family came from Clarke County, a little west of there. Grandma always told us that's where her family had been for five generations before her, and that's where she was going to stay. I'm sure that's where Angeline was from."

Annie stood up. "You two had better hurry if you're going to get to the bank before it closes."

"We two?" Alice put her hands on her hips. "And just where are you off to?"

"You can drop me off at the library." Annie grabbed her purse. "We'll meet up at The Cup & Saucer when you're finished at the bank."

~ 19 ~

Less than half an hour later, Annie hurried into The Cup & Saucer and slid into the booth next to Alice.

"Did you two get everything taken care of?"

Mary Beth nodded. "I'll be able to sleep tonight, and I know I wouldn't have with all that ..." She glanced around and lowered her voice. "... with all that jewelry. It's all locked up in the bank until I can get it appraised and figure out what to do next. I don't guess the whole town needs to know about it."

Alice laughed. "They'll know soon enough, I suppose. What about you, Annie? You look like you're about to burst."

Annie wanted to bounce up and down in her seat. "I'm so excited, I probably look like some kind of mental case at this point. I don't know why I didn't think of it before, though."

"What?" Alice and Mary Beth asked at the same time, and then both of them laughed.

Annie couldn't help joining them. "I told you awhile ago that I looked up your great-great-grandparent's marriage in the Fairfax County, Virginia, marriage records. I looked at the same time to see if Geoffrey Whyte had married anyone before he died. Elopements, especially in wartime, aren't uncommon."

Mary Beth caught her breath. "And?"

"Nothing. Not at the time."

"Not at the time?" Alice repeated, narrowing her eyes.

"Then Mary Beth mentioned that back then her family, including Angeline, was from Clarke County, not Fairfax County. If she and Geoffrey did elope, especially if he wanted to keep it secret from his controlling mother, of course they wouldn't get married in his home county. What would be more natural than for them to marry in Angeline's?" Annie put the print out on the table in front of Mary Beth. "They were married on March 6, 1861, in Berryville, Virginia, in Clarke County."

"That's wonderful!" Alice exclaimed, her eyes alight.

Mary Beth stared at the page, blank-faced, not saying anything.

"They were married, Mary Beth." Annie reached across the table and shook her friend by the forearm. "They were married. Even if she didn't know it was there, everything Geoffrey had would have been legally hers once he died. That means it's yours. It's all yours!" She glanced around with a self-conscious giggle and then lowered her voice. "There will probably be some legal considerations, maybe some taxes."

Alice rolled her eyes. "There are always taxes."

"But I don't think anyone can claim it's not yours now," Annie continued, "especially since it's been in your family's possession for the past one hundred and fifty years."

"That's great." Mary Beth smiled tightly. "But let's not get too excited until we find out if it's really worth anything."

*   *   *   *

The next day, Mary Beth arranged for an appointment with a certified jewelry appraiser in Portland. Ian agreed to go with her.

"I'm just going along to make sure there's no trouble," Ian said, a big smile on his face. Mary Beth was glad to have him. It was a little disturbing to know she might be carrying thousands of dollars worth of antique jewelry around with her.

The appraiser—a Mrs. Banks—was approximately Mary Beth's age and looked more like she should be teaching Sunday School than dealing with expensive jewelry. But by the time she was through measuring and weighing and examining everything Mary Beth had brought, it was obvious she knew her business and did her job well.

"Now, as soon as I have the appraisal written up," Mrs. Banks said, "I'll mail it to you."

"Oh."

Mary Beth knew her disappointment must be plain to see.

Mrs. Banks smiled gently. "I know. Everyone thinks I can just come up with a number right away, but it's just not that easy. Especially with a lovely piece like this. I'll have to come up with comparables and compile all the information before I can give you a reasonable appraisal."

"Then you don't know yet if they're real."

"If they're real? Bless you, dear—of course they're real!" The appraiser's eyes twinkled. "I won't quote you a figure yet because it would just be a guess at this point, but I don't think you'll be disappointed. For now, you'd better get those back into your safe-deposit box."

Ian took Mary Beth's arm, grinning at her. "You all right?"

Mary Beth could only nod, and her hands trembled as she put the jewelry back into the little zippered bag she had brought them in. Then she put the bag into her purse and took out the keys to her SUV. Somehow she managed to thank Mrs. Banks, and then she made her way to the door.

With a chuckle, Ian took the keys from her hand. "I think you ought to let me drive us back to Stony Point."

* * * *

A few days later, Annie answered her telephone.

"Annie, it's Mary Beth. Do you think you and Alice could come over for a little while?" Her voice was breathless and unsteady and unnaturally high.

"Is anything wrong?"

"I—" Mary Beth laughed nervously. "I got the letter from the appraiser."

"What does it say?"

"Uh, I haven't opened it yet."

"Mary Beth!"

"I just can't make myself. Not by myself. Do you think you and Alice could come over?"

Annie laughed. "You silly thing! Let me give her a call. Either *we'll* be right over, or *I'll* come alone."

Annie hung up and immediately called Alice.

"Right now?" Alice complained. "I've got a Divine Décor party to get to."

"You don't have just a minute or two? Mary Beth just got

her appraisal, and she doesn't want to open it by herself."

"Well why didn't you say so? Listen, if you think she'll drop you back home later, I'll drive us both over and then head straight to my party from there."

"Sounds like a plan, Alice. I'll be right out."

A few minutes later they were at Mary Beth's, hurrying breathlessly to her door. Mary Beth almost dragged them inside.

"I can't stand it." She held up a white envelope with a professional-looking logo on it. "I'm dying to know what it says, and I just can't make myself open it. What if it's a hundred thousand dollars? What if it's two?"

Annie sat her down on the couch, and then she and Alice sat on either side of her. "The best thing to do is to just open it and find out. Whatever it is, it's more than you have. Just take a deep breath and open it up."

Mary Beth screwed her eyes closed and shook her head. "You open it."

"It's yours, Mary Beth," Annie told her. "I think you should—"

"Oh, for goodness sake—I'll open it!" Alice grabbed the envelope and slid her fingernail under the flap. She had to tear it a little to get it all the way open, and then she handed the contents to Mary Beth. "There."

Again Mary Beth shook her head and passed the papers over to Annie.

There were three or four pages of information about the jewels, the weight and number and quality of the various stones and their settings, the qualifications of the appraiser, the methods she used to reach a value, but that's not what any of them wanted to know right then. Finally Annie found what she was looking for: the value.

"Mary Beth," she whispered. Then she swallowed and looked again. "Mary Beth, they appraised it at five sixty-five."

Mary Beth's mouth dropped open and her eyes filled with disappointment. "Five hundred and sixty-five dollars? I thought—"

"No, Mary Beth, five hundred and sixty-five *thousand*. Five hundred and sixty-five thousand dollars!"

For a moment there was only a stunned silence.

Then Alice whooped and started dancing around the room. "No more Burly Boy! No more Burly Boy!"

Tears filled Mary Beth's eyes, and she threw her head back and laughed. "No more Burly Boy!"

After a cup of strong coffee and a few hugs, Mary Beth was finally able to look over the documentation from the appraiser.

"It's true. It's really, really true. I guess I'll have my hands full getting the jewelry sold and arranging to buy the shop and everything."

"I don't know if they can sell something like that over-night," Annie said, "but I bet you can find someone who can handle it quickly for you."

Alice grinned. "I just wonder what that Frank Sanders would say now if he knew what that jewelry is worth. He'd be spitting nails."

Annie giggled, but Mary Beth could only shake her head.

"I just can't believe it. It's too amazing."

Annie squeezed her hand. "It's an answer to prayer."

"And don't forget," Alice said, "no more Burly Boy!"

To that, Annie and Mary Beth added a hearty amen.

*   *   *   *

Before long, Alice had to hurry off to her Divine Décor party, and Mary Beth drove Annie home.

"I still can't believe it," Mary Beth said for probably the tenth time that evening. "It's a pity though. Geoffrey provided for Angeline, and she never knew about it. Think how much easier her life could have been if she had been able to have the money this would have brought. It was always here for when she needed it."

Annie felt a sudden surge of joy bubbling up inside her. "Or maybe you could think that this was put here for when *you* would need it most."

"Oh Annie." Mary Beth bit her lip. "Do you think …?"

"Of course it's a miracle. You deserve to have something good finally happen to you after all you've been through lately, with the shop and the break-in and your sister …" Her *sister.* They pulled up to a stop sign, and Annie put her hand on Mary Beth's arm. "Wait."

Mary Beth glanced at the empty intersection. "What's wrong?"

"Melanie." Annie felt as if her birthday balloon had just burst. "I hadn't even thought about her before."

"Oh." Mary Beth sat at the intersection for a while and then finally nudged the gas pedal. "Well, if the jewelry does belong to our family, it belongs to both of us equally—Mel and me. That's what Mom's will said as far as dividing her property, so I have to think it would be the same for this. It's only right."

"I'm sure that's true. Won't that change things? As far as you buying the building and everything?"

Mary Beth shrugged. "I don't suppose there's much I can do about it."

And Mary Beth didn't say anything for a long while after that.

"What are you thinking?" Annie asked as they pulled up at Grey Gables. "Melanie still?"

With a rueful smile, Mary Beth nodded. "At this point, I'd rather just mail her a check and be done with it."

"Well, once you sell it at a reasonable price, I don't see how she could object."

"Oh, you don't know Melanie. She would be sure she could have gotten a better price. And no doubt I paid too much in commissions to whoever brokered it for us. How did I know I wasn't cheated? How did she know I wasn't cheating *her*?"

Annie shook her head. "Surely she wouldn't think that of you. Would she?"

Mary Beth chuckled. "No, I don't really think she would. But I'm sure I'll do something wrong in handling the deal."

"Why not let *her* do it then?" Annie asked.

"That's the thing. If I ask her to take care of it, she'll tell me how busy she is and ask me why I can't handle the simplest of business affairs. Either way, she's not going to be happy."

"You know, some people never are," Annie said, "and you'll drive yourself crazy trying to make them happy. All you can do is do your best and not let them keep *you* from being happy."

Mary Beth smiled as she got out of the car. "I think that's the best advice I've heard all day."

* * * *

There was nothing else to do and no use in putting it off. Mary Beth would just have to call Melanie and tell her about the jewels. She sat down on the couch and closed her eyes, breathing deeply and thinking peaceful thoughts.

I will be pleasant and not easy to upset. All I have to do is let her know what's going on. We don't have to decide what to do right this minute. We can figure out the details once we know more. I'm not going to be intimidated by my own sister.

She took a deep breath and punched Melanie's number into the phone.

"Hello?"

"Hi, Melanie. It's Mary Beth. Do you have a minute to talk?"

"Only a minute. I have a premiere to go to." Melanie's voice was brisk and businesslike. "What's on your mind?"

"You remember the things Grandma Marie said were passed down to her from her grandmother? The clock and the desk and things?"

"Yes. Very nice in their way, of course, but you know I don't like that fussy, old-fashioned stuff. And no, I don't have any interest in buying any of it to bail you out. I'm sure there are all kinds of dealers around, though I doubt what you have would be enough to fix the mess you've gotten yourself into."

"I'm not asking you for anything, Mel, I just wanted you to know something. I had the clock in being repaired and—"

"Mother gave all that stuff to you when she moved into that old folks' home, didn't she? Goodness knows, I didn't want them. Anyway, they're yours, and so is the responsibility for their upkeep. I know getting something like that done is expensive, but you should have gotten an estimate before you agreed to the repairs. I can't really do anything about that, can I?"

"Melanie, I'm not asking—"

"It's amazing to me that you've stayed in business even this long. You don't have much of a head for practical matters, do you?"

Mary Beth said nothing. She merely waited.

"Mary Beth? Are you there? Can you hear me?"

"I can hear you, Melanie. Can you hear me?"

"Well for crying out loud, why didn't you answer me? I told you already that I'm in a hurry."

"I was waiting for you to give me a chance to say something."

From the other end of the line, Mary Beth heard an impatient little huff.

"Go ahead."

"I just wanted you to know that there was something hidden in the clock that's worth a lot of money. It's been in there for over a hundred and fifty years. Mom couldn't have known about it. Even our great-great-grandmother who was meant to have it didn't know about it."

"What do you mean by 'worth a lot of money'?" Melanie sneered. "A thousand dollars?"

"No. A lot more than that. A whole lot more. Five hundred and sixty-five thousand."

Melanie didn't say anything. "What ... what exactly is it?" she asked finally.

"A really amazing necklace with pearls and rubies and diamonds, and earrings and a ring to match. It's all gorgeous."

"And why are you telling me this? To gloat?"

"I just wanted you to know that half of it is yours. We're all that's left of our great-great-grandmother Angeline's descendants. To me, that means it belongs to both of us equally."

Again Melanie was silent.

"Mel?"

"Mother gave that clock and all those other things to you." Melanie's voice was very soft now and not very steady. "I'd say anything inside one of them belongs to you. After all, she left the business to me."

"She didn't know there was something in the clock. I'm sure she would have wanted us both to have it, if she had known."

"You might be able to get it all awarded to you, if you went to court."

"Melanie!" Mary Beth shook her head, not knowing whether to laugh or cry. Melanie would never understand her. It was no use. "I don't want to go to court. Not over this or anything. I'm not trying to keep all of it. I think it's right that we both share it."

"What about your shop? If you had all of the money, you

could buy it, and your troubles would be over."

Mary Beth chuckled. "Troubles are never really over. Not in this world. And yes, if I had all the money, I could probably buy the whole building and let the theater next door pay me rent. That way I'd have enough to stay afloat during the lean times, no matter how the shop does. But it doesn't belong to me. At least I don't think it should. It belongs to both of us. You're welcome to have it appraised by someone yourself if you don't think my appraiser gave us a fair value."

"I'll certainly do that." Melanie's voice was taut and businesslike again. "Now, if that's all, I have a premiere to get to. Goodbye."

There was a click and then a dial tone. Mary Beth put her phone back in the charger and sat there for a long time, just watching the dusk turn to pitch black.

⁓ 20 ⁓

As promised, Melanie sent her own appraiser to look over the jewelry. His estimate of the value of the jewels was fairly close to the one Mary Beth had gotten from Mrs. Banks and which seemed quite satisfactory to the company that now insured the collection. Mary Beth had also consulted an attorney regarding the legal and tax ramifications of the find. She could hardly believe it was worth over a half-million dollars.

It was too bad she couldn't buy just the portion of the building that housed A Stitch in Time and not worry about the part where the theater was. Her part of the treasure would be enough to cover just the shop. But Mr. Huggins needed to sell the whole thing. Mr. Li, who rented the theater, had no way of buying that part of the building himself.

"If I can't buy both, Mr. Huggins will have no choice but to sell the whole thing to the Burly Boy people," she told the members of the Hook and Needle Club on the last Tuesday of the month, "and I can't buy both."

"Oh Mary Beth, what will you do?" Peggy wadded her appliquéd quilt block in her lap, almost pricking herself with her needle. "I thought will all that money ..."

Mary Beth got up to pick up the mail that had come through the slot in the front door. "It's still six days until the end of the month. I'll have to see what happens. Meanwhile,

I've looked around a little bit. There's a little storefront in Pleasant Point that I could probably afford. The money does make it easier."

"Pleasant Point," half a dozen voices moaned at once.

"That's miles away," Gwen said. "We couldn't be running over there all the time like we do now."

"I know I couldn't come for meetings," Peggy said. "I'd no sooner get there than I'd have to come right back to work."

Mary Beth dredged up a cheerful smile as she flipped through the day's bills and advertisements. "I know it's not as good as being right next door to The Cup & Saucer, Peggy. Sometimes we ..."

In with the rest of the mail was a letter from Mr. Huggins. She had read through half of it before she realized what it was saying.

"What is it, Mary Beth?" Annie looked concerned. "Are you OK?"

"It's from Mr. Huggins. He says he has a buyer for the theater property if I'm willing to buy this part of it myself." She sank down into her chair in the sewing circle. "And the price is a little less than I thought it might be."

All the ladies started talking at once, but Mary Beth didn't hear much of what they were saying. There was more in the letter.

"Will you have enough for it?" Annie asked. "You look worried."

Mary Beth glanced up at her, knowing she must be pale as a ghost. There was no way any blood could possibly make it past the tightness in her throat into her face.

"I just can't—"

She handed the letter to Annie, who scanned it briefly.

"Oh Mary Beth. It's wonderful."

The other ladies crowded around. "What? *What?*"

"'The proposed buyer of the other part of the property,'" Annie read, "'is looking for a small investment. The buyer would like to continue renting that part of the property to the Bijou Theater but doesn't want to be involved in property management. The buyer would like to know if you ...'" Annie looked up at Mary Beth. "'... if you would be interested in managing the theater property in exchange for a percentage of the rental.' That couldn't take very much work, could it?"

"No. No, Mr. Huggins says Mr. Li who runs the theater is a wonderful tenant. There are never any problems. He always pays on time." Mary Beth couldn't keep a tremor out of her voice. "Read the rest, Annie. The last part."

"'If this is something that interests you, please let me know as soon as possible, and I will arrange a meeting between us and the proposed buyer of the other part of the property, Ms. Melanie Martinelli.'"

Mary Beth buried her face in her hands and wept. It was as close to an apology as her sister was ever likely to give.

* * * *

Mary Beth had to wait until she had closed the shop and had gone home before she was sure she could call Melanie to discuss the Mr. Huggins's letter. She knew her sister didn't like anyone to gush, and that's what she felt like doing every time she thought about what Melanie had done.

Melanie picked up the phone on the first ring. "Hello?"

Her voice was as crisp and businesslike as it had been the last time Mary Beth had spoken to her.

"Hi. It's Mary Beth again. Have I caught you at a bad time?"

"No, it's ... it's not a bad time. I just got in. For once, I'm going to have a quiet evening at home, alone."

"That sounds nice."

"It sounds wonderful." Melanie paused for a second. "I think it's time I slowed down a little, you know?"

"Maybe you should take some time off. Maybe visit family or something."

Mary Beth let the subtle invitation hang there for a moment, but Melanie evidently wasn't quite ready for that.

"What are you doing tonight?"

"Not much," Mary Beth told her. "I just got home myself, and a quiet evening sounds great to me too. I wanted to let you know I got a letter from Mr. Huggins about the property. Are you really sure this is what you want to do? I mean, owning our little one-screen theater isn't exactly what I'd call glamorous."

"It's what I want to do only if you'll agree to manage the property. Mr. Huggins said the tenant is very reliable."

"That's what I've heard as well. But you don't need to cut me in on your profits. I'm just next door. I can see to things for you pretty easily. It's the least I can do since you'll be making it possible for me to keep my shop." Mary Beth laughed. "And you'll be sparing all of us a twenty-four-hour Burly Boy's Burger Barn."

"I suppose I will be bringing progress in your little town to a grinding halt," Melanie said with an overly dramatic sigh, but Mary Beth could hear the smile in her voice too. "But then again, being stuck somewhere in the *Leave It to Beaver* era is part of the appeal of the place, isn't it? I mean—to some people."

"*Some people* love it here and are very happy to be able to stay. And I mean that sincerely. Thank you."

"Just a business transaction," Melanie said, her voice again brisk. "Besides, I know we're both planning to leave everything to Amy. She might have plans of her own for the place one day."

"Yes, I suppose she might."

"I told her about it the other night," Melanie said abruptly. "About buying the place."

"Oh really? What did she say when you called her."

"She called me. She just wanted to talk, and we did for a while. I ... I thought it was kind of nice."

Mary Beth felt a smile tug at her lips. "I'm glad."

"I suppose you got her to do that."

"We did talk about it," Mary Beth admitted, "but she wouldn't have done it if she didn't want to."

"Maybe. Maybe not. Anyway, I told her about buying the theater up there and everything. I mean, it was really her idea in the first place, and I thought it would be nice for her to know we cooperated on something for once in our lives. It's going to be strictly business though." Melanie's voice lost the touch of softness that had crept into it. "That's the only way to handle family-related investments. Everything has to be aboveboard and set down in writing."

"That suits me," Mary Beth said, making her own voice businesslike. There was only so much mush Melanie could tolerate in one evening.

"And you will accept a percentage of the rental in payment for managing the theater property. I expect you to sign a contract so there won't be any misunderstandings that this is strictly a business arrangement."

Mary Beth could only nod. That little extra was Melanie's way of making sure her sister was taken care of.

"Are you there, Mary Beth?"

"Yes," Mary Beth squeaked, and then she cleared her throat. "Yes, I'm here. And yes, I'll be happy to sign whatever agreement you want."

"Well, I'll have my attorneys see to everything, and we'll get it taken care of at the same time we do the closing, if that's not a problem."

"That'll be fine."

"Well, goodnight then."

"Goodnight." Mary Beth paused. "And Mel?"

"Yes?"

"I love you."

Mary Beth heard the line click and then a dial tone, but she was almost sure that, right before then, she heard a soft, "Love you too."

*   *   *   *

The following Saturday night, Frank Sanders showed up late for his usual poker game. He'd had a rotten day at the shop, and now his car was giving him fits. All he needed was to lose a bundle in tonight's game to round things off.

The battered round table and mismatched chairs were the best features of Dave Avery's cluttered den, but at least the place was comfortable. More importantly, Dave's wife didn't seem to object to having visitors most Saturday nights, and Dave and his friends had a regular place to play.

Once he was inside, Sanders shut the door behind him. "Sorry I'm late, guys."

Squinting through his thick glasses, Eric nodded a welcome, but Scott was too busy raking in his winnings to do more than glance up and grumble, "About time."

Murphy lumbered to his feet and made a low bow. "His Majesty arrives."

Frank responded with a pained smile. "Funny."

"Hey, Frank." Dave pushed back the empty chair next to him and lifted one bushy eyebrow. "We thought maybe you got hit by a bus."

Frank dropped into his seat and anted up with the others. "Wouldn't surprise me."

"Now you get to pay up on our little agreement." Dave grinned as he dealt Sanders in. "Big bucks, remember?"

"Yeah, uh, that deal I was hoping for didn't quite pan out. You're going to have to settle for the usual until I win the lottery or something."

Sanders picked up his cards. Queen, king and ten of diamonds. Four of spades. Eight of clubs. He and three of the others tossed a few bucks into the pot. Eric folded.

"Cards?" Dave asked.

"Three," said Murphy.

"Yeah, three," said Scott.

Frank put the eight and the four facedown on the table and slid them over to Dave. "Give me two."

"All right." Dave dealt them their cards. "And the dealer takes one."

Eric chuckled. "Looks like it might be Dave who's about to win the lottery."

Dave grinned as he looked at his hand. "Yeah, that'd be the life. A big windfall, no matter where it's from, sure wouldn't hurt. I read this morning about some woman up the coast who found half a million in old jewelry. It'd been in the family for years, and nobody knew about it."

Sanders kept his jaws clamped together and didn't look up. Why couldn't stuff like that ever happen to him? Even when he knew he was onto a sure thing, it always seemed to go wrong.

He picked up one of the cards he'd just been dealt. Ace of diamonds. His pulse picked up its pace, but he kept his face carefully blank. Maybe at last he was going to have something good happen. Scott and Murphy both threw in their hands in disgust.

"Heh heh, dumb luck wins every time, doesn't it?" Eric shook his head. "Still, how could she not know? I mean, if those jewels were sitting around all that time. Must've had a pretty stupid bunch of relatives. Where was it?"

Sanders picked up his last card, still not looking at it. *Jack of diamonds. Be the jack of diamonds.*

"It was in the bottom of some old clock of hers," Dave said.

Sanders froze. "What?"

"Yeah. The paper says it'd been there since before the

Civil War. Can you imagine? Now the old biddy's set for life."

Frank's fingers squeezed into a fist, crumpling his still unseen card. "Wh—where was this?"

Dave shrugged. "I dunno. Somewhere up the coast." He rummaged in a pile of newspaper on the floor next to him and then tossed one section onto the table in front of Sanders. "Read for yourself."

Sanders's eyes started to burn. *STONY POINT WOMAN FINDS ANTIQUE TREASURE.* And there was a picture of that Brock woman standing there holding a fortune in diamonds and pearls and rubies with that miserable clock on the mantel behind her. He scanned the article.

Mary Beth Brock of Stony Point never knew there was a fortune in the family ... hidden in the clock for over 150 years ... clues were hidden in various antique items passed down from her great-great-grandmother Angeline... solved with the help of her friends Annie Dawson and Alice MacFarlane ... jewels were appraised at more than a half-million dollars.

More than a half-million dollars.

Sanders closed his eyes, wondering if he was going to burst out laughing or just be sick. He'd had it in his hands. Over half a million bucks right in his hands, and he'd let a bunch of old women con him out of it. Of all the—

He wiped the cold sweat off his upper lip and realized he still had that last card crumpled in his fist. Finally, he looked at it. Nine of hearts. A useless old nine of hearts.

Murphy elbowed him. "Hey, you gonna play or meditate?"

Sanders threw his hand onto the table. "I fold."

"Come to papa," Dave crowed, raking in his winnings.

Eric started shuffling the deck. "Must be all kinds of stuff squirreled away in clocks and tins and things all over the country. Old furniture sometimes has a lot of hidey-holes. You see much of that in your business, Frank? ... Frank?"

Sanders tossed in his ante. "Shut up and deal."

*   *   *   *

"You're all still here!"

Mary Beth hurried into A Stitch in Time carrying a large white envelope with the name of a local title company blazoned in red across it. It was fairly bursting with papers. So much had happened in the weeks since Annie had found that first little key.

Annie pulled her over into the circle of chairs where she and the other members of the Hook and Needle Club had been packing up their things.

"We weren't about to leave until you got back. How did it go?"

Before Mary Beth could answer, the bell on the front door jingled, and Ian Butler hurried in.

"I hope I'm not interrupting your meeting, but I saw you were back, and I thought I'd come over and congratulate you. Everything go as planned?"

Mary Beth patted the bulging envelope. "It's all legal. I own the shop, Melanie owns the theater, and I have no more money troubles." She grinned. "*If* I'm careful. Oh, and Mr. Huggins said his wife is doing really well now. She had her surgery two weeks ago, and rehab is going great. He looked a lot less worried than I've seen him in a long, long time."

"Poor old Frank Sanders. He had the treasure in his

hands all along." Ian chuckled as he sat down on the arm of one of the overstuffed chairs. "If he could only see you now."

"He should be in jail," Peggy grumbled, but Mary Beth only smiled.

"He really didn't do anybody much harm but himself, and I probably would never have found the jewels if not for him. And Mandy's little acting job more than repaid me for that broken window. It seems like everything that was meant to hurt me turned out to be for my good. I can't complain about that."

"And I can't complain about the nice little chat I had with the corporate planner of SLR & FFH, Ms. McMillan." Ian winked at Annie. "I did have a chance to let her know Mr. Huggins and Stony Point regret that there will not be a new Burly Boy's Burger Barn on Main Street."

Alice giggled. "I suppose she wasn't too happy about that."

"I think she was more astonished than anything," Ian said. "She made it pretty clear that she's used to getting her own way. I guess she'll get over it."

Annie smiled at him. "I'm so glad. I love Stony Point just as it is."

"Me too!" Mary Beth felt like throwing a party or tap-dancing across the front counter of the store. She contented herself with giving Annie a hug. "Me too!" she exclaimed again for emphasis.

Annie returned the hug and then hesitated. "And how was Melanie?"

Mary Beth couldn't help beaming at her. "We had a nice talk after all the paperwork was done. She and Amy are going to meet me for lunch next week when they're in Portland. Melanie and I are not best friends yet, but I think we're heading in the right direction."

"It's a miracle."

Mary Beth gave her friend another big hug. "A miracle that started with a little key in Annie's attic."